Woodland Dell's Secret

Books by Carrie Bender

Miriam's Journal
A Fruitful Vine
A Winding Path
A Joyous Heart
A Treasured Friendship
A Golden Sunbeam

Miriam's Cookbook

Dora's Diary
Birch Hollow Schoolmarm
Lilac Blossom Time
Beyond Mist-Blue Mountains

Whispering Brook Series
Whispering Brook Farm
Summerville Days
Chestnut Ridge Acres
Hemlock Hill Hideaway
Woodland Dell's Secret
Timberlane Cove

Woodland Dell's Secret

Carrie Bender

Herald
Press

Scottdale, Pennsylvania
Waterloo, Ontario

Library of Congress Cataloging-in-Publication Data
Bender, Carrie, date.
Woodland Dell's Secret / Carrie Bender.
        p. cm.—(Whispering Brook series ; 5)
ISBN 0-8361-9169-2 (alk. paper)
    l. Amish—Fiction. 2. Pennsylvania—Fiction. I. Title.
PS3552.E53845 W66 2001
813'.54—dc21   2001024365

The paper used in this publication is recycled and meets the minimum requirements of American National Standard for Information Sciences—Permanence of Paper for Printed Library Materials, ANSI Z39.48-1984.

This story is fiction, but true to Amish life. Any resemblance to persons living or dead is coincidental. Scripture is adapted from KJV. Other "Notes and Credits" are near the end of the book.

Contents

1. Spring Delights 7
2. A Wild Daydream 13
3. The Campfire 20
4. A Test of Bravery 27
5. Pancakes and Promises 33
6. Terror in the Dark 39
7. A Night for Mulling 45
8. Silly or Nice? 51
9. The Storm 57
10. A Varmint Attack 63
11. The Woodland Stroll 69
12. Lost in the Woods 75
13. A Hospital Visit 80
14. How the Wind Blows 85
15. Tender Loving Care 91
16. Florabelle 98
17. A Peacekeeper 105
18. Two Escapees 110

19. The Fugitive 116
20. Ebony in Stride 122
21. The Long Way Home 129
22. Real Luxury 136
23. The Born Naturalist 142
24. Dannie's Return .148
25. As an Alien 154
26. Home to Stay 160
27. The Family Picnic 165

Notes and Credits 173
The Author 175

1

Spring Delights

NANCY Petersheim picked up a walking stick she had found beside the cow path. She was heading through the buttercup-filled meadow to fetch the cow for the evening milking. The spring grasses were lush and green, and a robin cheerily sang from the rose thicket behind the house.

Her brother Omar had put up a purple martin birdhouse. To their delight, not many days had passed until the graceful warbling birds had moved in and set up housekeeping. She could hear their cheerful gurgling and warbling now, as they dived and swooped for insects, or just sang from the porch of their house.

Because Nancy was fetching the cow half an hour earlier than usual, the cow was still grazing peacefully way over on the other side of the pond. That meant a long walk for Nancy, but she didn't mind. She loved these morning and evening rambles down into the meadow, with fragrant wild cherry or apple blossoms (in season) floating down from the trees, and the sweet chorus of birdsong reverberating from the woods and dells at the base of Hemlock Hill.

Nancy sighed as she surveyed the beautiful scenery and lovely springtime sights and sounds all around her. "I'd better enjoy all this while I can," she reminded herself out loud. "When Omar gets married, he won't need me for his housekeeper anymore. Then I'll have to move back home to Mamm and Daed. I'll sure miss this neighborhood, especially my good friends Sally and Andrew Fisher.

"I doubt that it'll be more than a year and a half until Omar and Sally get married. Knowing how fast time flies, I might as well start preparing myself to leave."

On such a lovely spring evening, it was hard to stay doleful for long. Nancy's spirits quickly revived. Omar was cutting hay in the west field. The clatter of the mowing machine, pulled by the two plodding workhorses, drifted across the meadow, along with sweet fragrance from the freshly mown clover field.

Beside the small brooklet of spring water that trickled into the pond, a cottontail rabbit suddenly sprang out of a bed of ferns and bounded away to hide in the thickets. Nancy stopped by the stream, remembering how the slope had looked just a short time earlier, when the bluebells were blooming. The solid bed of small sweet-smelling flowers had been the prettiest shade of blue she had ever seen.

Each stage of spring had its own beauty—spring peepers in chorus; freshly plowed fields; blooming daffodils, hyacinths, and tulips; meadows greening up; and songsters arriving—always something new and wonderful to delight the senses.

Nancy milked the cow and turned her out to pasture again. By then, Omar had finished mowing the clover field and was bringing the horses in to the barn to unhitch.

"I made you some sandwiches and chocolate milk," Nancy told him. "I knew you wouldn't take the time to come in for supper before calf-feeding time anyway."

"Good!" Omar's smile crinkled the corners of his eyes as he unbuckled the horses' harnesses. "Spring sure is a busy time of year. I always seem to be a step behind. But I've got good news. Dannie's coming out here in a few days!

"This morning Mary sent Nancy Ann out to the fencerow with a note. They had a letter from Mamm today. She wrote that since school's out, Dannie is eager to come and be our *Gnecht* (hired man). We sure can use him around here. He'll take turns helping out here and at Jacob's place."

"So! That's good news." Nancy smiled to herself as she gathered the calf buckets in preparation for feeding the veal calves, while Omar mixed the milk replacer and ate his snack.

She was thinking, *I wonder if Dannie will find him-*

self another pet this summer. Two years ago, Dannie had tamed a little raccoon. That summer had proved to be a turning point in his attitudes. The Petersheim family had taken Dannie into their home as a foster son after he was abandoned by his dad. At first Dannie had been rebellious and difficult. Then he sneaked off with his pet to the little cabin in the hemlock woods, on a knob at the back of Omar's farm.

Dannie's retreat in the woods had given him time out to realize the poor course he was taking. He had resolved to change his attitudes. Then their good friend and neighbor Ivor found him in the woods, and took him home to his wife, Helga, where he spent the night and the next day.

Dannie had come back home to Omar and Nancy, with new resolve to accept the friendship of these people giving him a home. By now, he was one of the family and seemed like a real brother to them. Even Nancy's sister Mary and her husband, Jacob, on a neighboring farm, wanted to see Dannie again.

Shortly before nine o'clock in the morning, two days later, a van turned into the lane at the Hemlock Hill Homestead. Dannie enthusiastically crawled out, carrying his duffel bag of clothes, his fishing rod, and a boxful of goodies that Mamm had sent along.

He set his things inside the kitchen door, greeted Nancy in his friendly way, and then was off in a flash, out the door and racing to the barn. There Omar was hitching up the horses to the hay rake, ready to head out to the field.

Nancy eagerly opened Mamm's box. Yes, here was

a letter from her, and Susie and Lydia had written, too. She eagerly devoured the contents of the letters, then went through the rest of the box. There was a loaf of homemade whole wheat bread, a box of sugar cookies, a jar of rhubarb jam, and a jar of homemade vegetable soup. Mamm's generosity never failed!

Nancy suddenly found herself swallowing hard. She loved being here and keeping house for Omar, but there were times when she was homesick for her parents, brothers, and sisters back home. She wished she could be two places at once.

"*Ya well* (yes, well), this will never do—moping around like this," Nancy chided herself. "I promised Sally I'd pick her up at ten, and it's nearly that time already!" She donned a clean apron and her bonnet, then hurried out to the barn to harness Dandy, the pony, and hitch him to the pony spring wagon.

A short time later, Nancy was driving in the Fishers' lane. Sally came out the walk, eager to ride with Sally to a greenhouse two miles away, to buy garden plants. Sally's brother, Andrew, waved from the doorway of the harness shop. Then they were off, out the lane in a flurry of gravel. Dandy was feeling frisky this morning, tossing his head, with his mane and tail flying in the breeze.

"Did I see a van pass our place, heading your way?" Sally asked. "I thought maybe your parents surprised you and came for the day, and we wouldn't be able to make the trip to the greenhouse after all."

"No, just Dannie. He's here for the summer—he wants to be both Omar's and Jacob's *Gnecht*. Perhaps they'll make a farmer out of him yet. He loves it."

"It's amazing how much that boy has changed," Sally marveled. "The last time I saw him, I couldn't believe he was the same boy. He's getting to be real handsome, too. Does he still have a soft spot in his heart for small animals, or injured creatures?"

"Probably. Mamm says he is of two minds, trying to decide whether to be a veterinarian or a farmer. For either job, he'd be working with animals." Nancy chuckled. "I wonder if these wishes are just a passing fancy. If he really has his heart set on it, I wouldn't be surprised if he'd pursue his dream until it's accomplished. He is that kind of fellow."

"Wouldn't that be something!" Sally giggled. "Doctor Dannie! *Unbegreiflich!* (unbelievable)."

This seems like old times, Nancy thought happily. *Now that Sally and Omar are going steady, she and I don't do things together as much. Maybe after we're sisters-in-law. . . .* Nancy sighed wistfully at the thought.

Deep down, she knew their days of carefree girlhood friendship were soon going to become a thing of the past, and she felt a twinge of regret. Nothing ever stayed the same. For all she knew, they would soon live a hundred miles apart.

"Oh well, maybe 'the best is yet to be,'" she told herself, trying to cheer herself up. "At least, Omar will be happy."

2

A Wild Daydream

BACK home, Nancy kicked off her shoes, took her box of greenhouse plants and a trowel, and headed for the garden. She loved to dig in the soft, rich soil, setting out tomato and pepper plants. Nancy knelt on the row of plastic she had laid to keep down the weeds as she set out sturdy-looking watermelon and cantaloupe plants. She had also bought petunias, marigolds, and geraniums for the flower beds.

Nancy hummed to herself as she worked at her favorite task, enjoying the warm sunshine and pleasant breezes, along with the joyous trilling of a robin in the rose thicket. At 11:30 she washed her hands at the garden pump and went in to the kitchen, to prepare a picnic lunch for Omar, Dannie, and herself.

She knew the men wouldn't want to quit raking hay until they were finished. This afternoon Jacob was coming over with his team to help with the baling. Nancy donned her sunbonnet and carried the lunch basket as she headed out the door. She was going to the back field, where they were raking hay near the woodland on Hemlock Hill.

Nancy noticed that Omar and Dannie had only a few more windrows to rake. She chose a shady spot in the woodland, by the small spring-fed water brook, and set down her basket. *This must be a dell*, she decided. She remembered looking up the word in the dictionary. The definition had been "a small secluded valley or glen, usually a wooded one."

This scenic spot fit that description perfectly. It was a small valley at the base of Hemlock Hill, secluded on three sides and wooded. She knew that the hemlock woods were full of dells like this, and shady rills, too. No wonder Dannie loved it.

Nancy sat on the grassy bank of the brook, listening to the birds' chorusing with energy and abandon. *How they must love springtime,* she mused. They sang as if they hadn't a care in the world, warbling ecstatically, with their whole heart. In the treetops, a squirrel flitted from branch to branch, scolding her noisily for invading his domain.

Nancy heard a twig snap from the path that wound up through the hemlock woods, and she whirled around. "Hello there!" a friendly voice called from the hillside. Making her way down the path came the plump, matronly figure of their elderly neighbor lady,

Helga, with their stately pet wolf at her side.

"Just my good luck to find you out here," Helga called. "This will save me quite a bit of walking." She made her way slowly down to Nancy, then lowered herself gingerly on a fallen log to rest. Wolf sank down beside her on the grassy bank.

"These old bones aren't as supple as they used to be," she groused. "My joints get to creaking, too, when I walk this far: But for right now, I'm better able to walk the distance than Ivor is.

"Did you notice how he walks with an awful limp this last half year or so? His knee is giving him a good deal of trouble. That's actually why I came over."

She shaded her eyes from the sun and glanced across the hayfield. "Is that Dannie I see there with Omar?" Her face lit up at the sight. "Just who I was hoping to see."

Helga waved her arm in a wide arc, and Omar and Dannie returned the wave. Wolf's ears perked up at the sight. Nancy thought that if wolves would wag their tails, this majestic beast surely would do so now. His usually aloof and regal-looking face wore an expression of utter benevolence and friendliness.

"I came to ask a favor of you folks," Helga continued. "Ivor is going to the hospital and having a knee replacement done. Omar had told us that Dannie would probably be here this summer. So we're wondering if he could come over every evening, about an hour before bedtime. We would like for him to help feed and care for our menagerie, then spend the night there, so I wouldn't need to be alone while Ivor is in the hospital.

"In the morning, he could leave again as soon as the chores are done. I know you folks are awfully busy in the spring, and we hate to ask. But we didn't know who else could do it, and we're quite fond of Dannie."

Nancy smiled. "I know Dannie will be eager to go. He thinks the world of you and Ivor, and I'm sure he would enjoy tending and feeding your animals. I suppose Omar will have to talk to Jacob about it, since Dannie was planning to help us both. But I'm sure they'll agree to let Dannie help you out while Ivor is in the hospital.

"That's what good neighbors are for," Nancy assured her. "We never know how soon we may be needing help ourselves. You'll be staying to share our picnic lunch, won't you?"

Helga was slowly getting to her feet, using Wolf as a support. "No, I must be on my way now. Ivor's waiting for me to eat lunch with him, and I want to stop at the spring for watercress. If I could stay, it would be lovely to eat and visit here, under the trees. Ivor and I used to do a lot of such picnicking when we were younger.

"Ya well, you talk it over, and when you've decided, maybe Dannie can come over and let us know. Ivor doesn't go to the hospital till next Monday. Come, Wolf." With a wave of her hand, the elderly woman and the shaggy beast made their way slowly up the path.

When Omar and Dannie joined Nancy at her chosen picnic spot, she told them what Helga had wanted. Dannie was all for it! Between mouthfuls of Mamm's vegetable soup, whole wheat bread, and lettuce sandwiches, he talked of how delightful that would be. He'd have an excuse to ramble through the hemlock woods morning and evening, and to care for Ivor's animals.

"That should work out all right," Omar agreed. "This morning I talked with Jacob at the fencerow. He told me his eleven-year-old nephew wants to came and help him this summer now after all. So we and Ivors can have Dannie all to ourselves." He grinned at his little brother.

Dannie tossed a few bread crumbs to the sparrows that were hopping around close to the tablecloth. "There's one thing I wish I'd have, and that's a horse I could ride," he said wistfully. "Think of all the time I'd save if I wouldn't need to walk all the way over to Ivors and back. I'm getting too big to ride Dandy—my feet nearly reach the ground. Do you think I could ride your horse, Beauty?"

Omar shook his head. "I'm afraid not. He's needed to help out in the fields and for driving on the road. We don't want to overwork him. Why don't you write to Daed and tell him you want a riding horse? He'd probably get you one if you asked."

"Say, that's just what I'll do," Dannie agreed enthusiastically. "A few years ago he offered to get me a colt if I wanted one, and I was too stubborn to accept the offer. I'm ashamed of myself now for the way I acted then."

"Ya well, we all make mistakes," Omar said

thoughtfully. "If we want to be forgiven for our mistakes, we must do the same for others." He leaned back against a tree trunk, pulling his hat down over his face to catch a few winks of shut-eye before returning to work.

While Nancy cleared away the meal, Dannie lay on the bank of the brook, watching the minnows darting here and there on the sandy bottom. This made him think of Bandit, his pet raccoon of two years ago. He wondered if the coon was still alive. Maybe he was even granddaddy already to a bunch of kits, and getting gray around the whiskers.

Dannie wished he could get another pet that would be as good a friend to him as Bandit had been. Right now his desire was for a horse. *If horses would still roam wild,* he thought wistfully, *I could capture one for myself.*

Daydreaming, he imagined himself out West, where wild mustangs still roamed the vast plains and the rugged mountains. He pictured himself standing on a mesa and gazing across the prairie to the next timbered mountain range, with the golden ball of sun rising up over the peaks.

In his mind's eye, he saw a group of wild horses, with manes and tails flying in the wind. They were gracefully trotting out of a mountain cove, with wild freedom. A shrill whinny from the leader stopped them in their tracks. Snorting loudly, with heads raised high, they stood gazing at Dannie warily, ready to take off again.

There was a gorgeous black stallion with a proudly

curved neck, head held high, and nostrils flaring, ready to give a signal of alarm. He saw shapely colts with glossy coats running beside their mothers, staring at Dannie curiously and suspiciously.

Then with another shrill and wavering cry from the stallion, the whole herd of splendid wild steeds wheeled. With a thunderous trampling of hooves, their tails streaming in the wind, they dashed off to the safety of the cove and disappeared from sight.

But ah! One of the two-year-old colts remained standing nearby, a beautiful pale gold one with a silky mane. He was gazing at Dannie and seemed to be unafraid. Dannie slowly walked toward him with a handful of grass. The colt reached for the grass and let Dannie stroke his smooth, glossy mane.

In his dream, Dannie saw himself leap on the colt's back in a flash. Then he was riding across the prairie. They were forever friends, never to be separated.

Dannie blinked his eyes, wondering who was shaking him.

"Time to get back to the field," Omar was saying. "We've both had a little nap."

Dannie jumped up. *So much for my dreams*, he thought wryly. *I guess I was born a hundred years too late. But I will have a horse of my own someday.*

3

The Campfire

ON Saturday morning Omar hitched Beauty to the spring wagon, to make a trip to the Shady Lane Tack Shop for some supplies. Dannie went along, hoping for a chance to have a chat with his friend Abie. It seemed like a long time since he'd seen him last.

Sure enough, there was Abie, energetically handling a big push brush and sweeping up the concrete area around the tie railing. "*Gude Mariye!* (good morning)." He greeted Dannie with a big smile. "My, it's good to see you again!"

Dannie jumped down from the spring wagon. "You too! Long time, no see. Wow! You must be expecting company, the way you're cleaning up around here. This place is spotless."

Abie nodded. "My aunt and uncle from Tennessee are coming. And their two boys, my cousins Seth and Alva, will be along. Seth is a year older than me, and Alva is a year younger. I thought it would be neat if we could camp out tonight, you know, take our sleeping bags and spend the night out in the meadow somewhere."

A sudden idea lit up Abie's face. "Say, Dannie, why don't you go along, too? We three could come over to Omar's place and find a place out somewhere in your hemlock woods! All we have here is a little grove in back of the barn, with a tiny little fenced-in meadow. It would be a lot more exciting in a real woods."

"*Wunderbaar!* (wonderful)." Dannie was all for it. "I'll go over to Ivor and Helga's place and ask for their permission. I'll make sure they'll chain up their Wolf in the shanty, or else we'll have to listen to his eerie howling. We could build a campfire and roast doggies, or fry the fish we catch."

"And explore," Abie added. "Isn't there a big dump somewhere in the woods? I can hardly wait. My oldest brother found a camera in a dump one time."

"You won't find any cameras there," Dannie assured him. "But there are a lot of interesting things to go and see in those woods, and the wildlife is plentiful."

Just then, Omar came out of the shop. As he untied Beauty, Dannie got his permission to sleep out and to use Omar's sleeping bag.

"We'll be over just before it gets dark," Abie called after them. "I'll bring the grub along."

"I'll supply a big cooler of mint tea," Dannie promised.

"And some of Nancy's cookies," Omar added. "Just make sure you'll get some sleeping done, so you won't be too sleepy to go to church tomorrow."

"We will," Dannie and Abie said in unison.

(The boys didn't realize how easily they would break their promise. The next day, at a neighbor's farmhouse, all four of the boys were seen dozing off during the three hours of services.)

"I wonder what Abie's cousins are like," Dannie said. "You don't happen to know Seth and Alva, do you?"

Omar shook his head. "No, I've never met them. I guess you'll have to wait till tonight to find out." He urged Beauty into a faster trot. "I have five hundred pounds of potatoes I'd like to plant today, and I'm depending on you to help. The weather's fine now, but they're predicting rain by Monday. The potatoes are already cut, so that will save us time."

"I'll do all I can to help," Dannie promised. As soon as they were home, he grabbed a bucket of cut potatoes, went to the woodshed for the hoe, and headed for Nancy's garden, as Omar had instructed him. Here he would plant a row of potatoes by hand. For planting out in the field, Omar would hitch Belle and Bo to the potato planter.

With the hoe, Dannie scratched a straight furrow the length of the garden. In that furrow, he chopped deeper holes a little farther apart than the length of his bare foot. The ground was in good shape, and the soft, dry soil pushed up between his bare toes.

The back screen door slammed as Nancy came out of the house, tying on her sunbonnet. "I'm ready to help now, too," she said, picking up the hoe and piling loose ground neatly over the potatoes that Dannie was dropping in the holes.

"I wonder what's going on over in the hemlock woods," Nancy said. "A while ago I heard barking from that direction. When I went to the window, I thought I glimpsed something running through the woods, perhaps a fox or a dog. And then Wolf began to howl like crazy. I may be mistaken, but I even thought I saw a person disappear into the shadows of that thick undergrowth on the other side of the picnic dell."

Dannie's eyes opened wide. "I hope there isn't a prowler in the woods that would make trouble for us boys tonight." He explained to Nancy about his and Abie's plans.

"Just be careful," Nancy warned. "If there really is someone in the woods, come up to the barn and sleep in the haymow. You'll be safe there."

Dannie nodded. But he was thinking, *Like fun! We won't let any old prowler scare us off. The woods belong to Ivor and Omar. We'll scare him off!*

After the evening chores were done, twilight was descending over the countryside. Dannie spied the bobbing figures of the three boys coming in the lane on scooters, each with a rolled-up sleeping bag under one arm, and paper sack in hand. Dannie grabbed his own knapsack, sleeping bag, and cooler, and hurried out the door to give them a proper welcome.

"Hi, Dannie," Abie called. "Come and meet my cousins. This tall one with dark hair is Seth, and the one with the glasses is Alva."

"*Wie geht's* (how are you)?" Dannie greeted them.

"We're fine and *eiferich* (eager) for fun," replied Seth.

Dannie shook hands with the boys, who seemed quite friendly and glad to see him.

"Are you ready to head for the woods?" Abie asked.

"Sure am. Let's start back right now while it's still light enough to gather firewood. I have matches and newspapers, too."

"And we have our flashlights," Abie said. "Do you think there's any chance of seeing deer?"

"There might be. But for that, we'd need strong spotlights. Maybe some other time we can go deer spotting, with Ivor's permission."

The hike back to the woods wasn't long. But by the time they reached the entrance to the woods, the four boys were chatting away like old friends, with all shyness gone.

"Thankfully, it's a warm summer evening," Seth observed, "a perfect night for sleeping out." A soft breeze swayed the hemlock branches overhead. From a distant treetop, a screech owl hooted in plaintive tones.

"I love these woods," Alva declared. "I mean, I'd love to go hunting here. This is more than just a grove of windbreak trees, like we have on our farm."

From somewhere over on the other side of the

woods, a dog began to whine and howl. Then suddenly all was quiet, as if a hand had been clapped over its mouth.

Dannie was glad he had told Ivor to chain Wolf in the shanty. The idea that there was a prowler in the woods unnerved him a bit. He decided to say nothing to the other boys, though, because he didn't want to alarm them. Perhaps it was just a camper like themselves.

"Listen to those spooky rustlings in the underbrush," Abie said. "What is it, mice or crickets, or what?"

"As long as it isn't snakes," Alva said quickly.

"Probably chipmunks and wood mice," Dannie said cheerfully. "Where would you like to camp, near a spring or a waterfall, or in a cabin?"

"Near the waterfall," Abie quickly decided. "I love the sound of falling water."

"Come this way, then." Dannie led the way along the trail. "Here's the old dump."

The boys shone their flashlights into the tangle of old tin and debris. "Nothing but a bunch of junk," Abie muttered. "The treasures must've been picked out long ago. Let's go on."

Dannie led the way, heading for the waterfall, dodging the vines and briars that grew out over the trail. "Here we are," he announced. The tinkling sound of the water cascading down over the rocks broke the stillness.

"Splendid!" Seth exclaimed. "Now, where's the firewood?"

"You'll have to help gather some fallen branches," Dannie told them. "I have a hatchet in my knapsack for chopping them up. Look, here's a level spot for our sleeping bags. I'll clear away the stones and twigs."

In a short time, the boys had a fire blazing cheerily in the near darkness and were sitting in a circle around it. They were holding long sticks for skewers, with hot dogs poked onto the ends of them, and were roasting them over the fire.

"Say, this is the life!" Alva remarked, retrieving his sizzling hot dog from the too-hot flame. "And to think that I almost chose not to come."

"Same here," Seth agreed. "I have some grand ideas for later. We'll have a night of adventure."

Abie grinned. "It should be good if these boys are behind it," he told Dannie. "There won't be a dull moment."

"I'm ready," Dannie said.

Just then a movement in the thickets caught his eye. Two gleaming yellow eyes stared straight at him for a moment, then disappeared into the shadows.

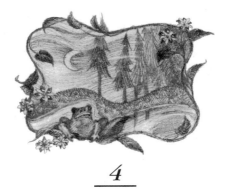

4

A Test of Bravery

DANNIE suddenly shivered, with dancing chills racing up and down his spine. Abie had just told a joke, which Dannie had missed, and the other boys were roaring with laughter. Dannie decided not to spoil their fun by mentioning those gleaming eyes. *It can't be anything very dangerous anyway,* he thought.

Seth threw another branch on the fire. It sputtered and sent blue-and-yellow flames and sparks upward, causing eerie, dancing reflections on the surrounding swaying leaves.

"Do you boys want to participate in the Midnight Haunt Test?" Seth asked. "It will be real scary and filled with thrills."

Dannie and Abie looked at each other. "Do you

know anything about this, Alva?" Abie asked. "Is it safe to get involved in it?"

Alva shrugged his shoulders. "Never heard of it."

"Of course not," Seth said scornfully. "I'm going to make it up myself. It's not for the timid or fearful—just for the brave and dauntless. Decide for yourselves whether or not you're game. The first to pass the test and be back here at the campfire gets a prize."

He drew a big Barlow pocketknife out of his pocket. "This is the prize. Of course, if no one passes the test, I get to keep the knife."

"Bah! I'm not helping," Alva said disgustedly. "You'll be sure to make the test too difficult so you can keep your knife."

"Oh no, I won't be that mean," Seth retorted. "I've got two knives like this. Teacher gave me one on the last day of school, and I already had one. I don't mind giving it away. Anyhow, the test won't be that difficult—just scary. It all depends on how brave you guys are, not how smart."

"All right, I'll take the test—if you'll let me make up a test of bravery for *you* to do," Dannie bargained. "Turnabout is fair play."

Seth hesitated. "All right," he finally agreed, laughing good-naturedly. "It would never do to chicken out after I challenged you guys. You've got to do your test first, though. And you'll have to wait till midnight, when it's pitch dark. Let's just sit here by the campfire and swap scary stories for awhile."

The night was velvety black by then. From down on the marsh came the poignant, deep-throated sound of bullfrogs croaking. The wind was whispering in the hemlock branches above, and from deep in the woods came the repetitious call of a saw-whet owl.

The glowing red embers of the banked fire cast an eerie glow on the surrounding hemlock branches as the boys took turns telling scary stories. They were enjoying the spine-tingling shivers they caused, even though they knew the tales were made up.

"Let's go swimming," Abie suddenly said, jumping up pulling off his shirt. He dived into the waterfall pool and came up gasping, swimming for the rock on the bank. "Whew! It's cold!"

He dived back in and began to swim vigorously, trying to get warm. In spite of seeing his chattering teeth, the rest of the boys couldn't resist following him. Soon all were tingling from the cold water.

"This creek must be spring-fed," Seth said. "I wish I'd have brought a towel." He also began to paddle and kick fast, trying to get warm.

Alva was the first to climb out. He piled more wood on the fire, stirred it up, then sat close to its warmth until he was dry enough to put his shirt back on. In a few minutes, the other boys joined him.

"We came too late to do any fishing," Seth remarked. "I'm hungry for a good pan-fried trout. What are we having for breakfast?"

"Pancakes," Abie told him. "Unless you'd rather have them now."

"Here are some cookies." Dannie got the bag out of his knapsack. "If you're too chilly to drink iced tea, we can heat some tea over the fire."

"Just the thing," Seth agreed. "And then, let's go for a walk, to see if any deer are out."

"You'll have to keep your mouth shut, though," Alva warned, "or else you'll scare them all away."

"Don't worry. I can sneak almost as silently as an Indian," Seth declared. "You'll see."

Later, as the four boys crept through the woods, they found out how difficult it was to tread noiselessly through brambles, vines, and dried leaves. Finally, though, their efforts were rewarded. The beams of their flashlights revealed a bewildered doe with a tiny spotted fawn at her side. The boys gasped in delight.

Both the doe's and the fawn's ears were perked up alertly, their dainty feet poised for flight. Their big luminous eyes were wide with fear as they faced the beams of the flashlights. The fawn suddenly wavered on its feet and gave a piteous little bleat. Instantly the doe turned and fled, leaping over a thicket and disappearing. The fawn ran around the thicket to join her.

"Wasn't that grand!" Abie breathed. "How I'd love to come back here some night with real spotlights. I bet we'd see dozens of deer."

"All right, it's time for the midnight scary test," Seth announced, breaking the spell the deer had cast. "Let's go back to the campfire."

When the boys were again seated around the fire, Seth told them about the test he had planned. "Here's what you'll have to do. When I say 'Go!' you go off into the woods at a fast walk, each in a different direction. When you hear me whistle again, you leave the trail and walk off into the thickets.

"Then you take off your shirts, blindfold yourselves with them, and turn around three times. The test is for you to find your way back to the campfire without taking off your blindfolds. I'll whistle every minute or so, and you can follow the direction of that sound to find your way to the campfire.

"The first one back without taking off his blindfold wins the knife. We'll see how good an Indian you'd make. If you chicken out by taking off your blindfold before you make it back to the campfire, you've failed the test."

Alva looked disgusted. "Is that all the better you can do?" he said scornfully. "That isn't even exciting. And think of all the poison ivy in the underbrush."

"Aw, c'mon, you can all jump back into the pool when you get back," Seth said. "I think you're just afraid."

Dannie spoke up. "I don't think that would be a fair contest. I know my way through these woods blindfolded, so I'd be sure to win. Why don't you join the other two, and I'll sit here by the fire and do the whistling. Remember, you agreed to take a test, too."

"Oh, all right." Seth reluctantly went along with Dannie's proposal when he saw that the others were insisting and wouldn't take no for an answer. He added gamely, "And if I fail the test, I promise to buy you each an ice-cream sundae sometime."

So at Dannie's signal, the three boys hurried off in the darkness. After what Dannie figured was about five minutes, he whistled shrilly, then waited to see what would happen. All seemed to be quiet in the woods now, except for the purring of the wind in the hemlock treetops and the call of the owl in the distance.

Suddenly a twig cracked sharply in the thickets to the left of him. Dannie whirled around. A tawny-colored animal whisked through a clearing, followed by a shadowy form leaping into the brush.

Dannie's heart suddenly raced with fear. There really was a prowler loose in the woods, likely watching them all evening. A sudden shiver ran up his spine, and he quickly drew closer to the campfire.

5

Pancakes and Promises

SQUATTING by the glowing embers of the campfire, Dannie suddenly remembered that he was supposed to whistle every now and then so the boys could find their way back. Summoning courage, he pursed his lips, sent a loud whistle reverberating through the woods, and waited as the quietness closed in again about him.

Half fearfully, Dannie peered into the darkness and shadows. He became aware of rustlings in the thickets, and he quickly threw more wood on the fire, watching the sparks fly and a blue flame leap to life. Suddenly he stiffened with fear. From not far away, a spine-tingling howl was filling the woods, starting on the eeriest, chillingest tones Dannie had ever heard.

"Awa-awa-ooh-awa-ooh-awa-oooo!"

Thinking that Wolf was chained in the shanty, Dannie was not expecting his howl. It had momentarily frightened him badly. Imagine the fright of blindfolded boys who had never heard it before! In a few moments, he heard sounds of yells and of scrambling and thrashing through the thickets. In a surprisingly short time, the three boys came crashing into the clearing, wide-eyed with fear and clutching their shirts.

"Wh—what was that?" Seth stuttered, sinking down beside the fire as if his legs refused to support him any longer.

Abie and Alva were trembling, too. "It sure sounded like a wolf," Alva declared. "Or maybe a coyote."

"It *was* a wolf," Dannie said. "I'm sorry I didn't tell you about the neighbors' pet wolf. I wonder how he got loose—he was supposed to be chained up."

"Whew!" Seth covered his head with his hands. "I thought I was being attacked by a whole pack of wolves."

"Hey, guys," Abie said in a weak, trembly voice. "Why don't we go down to Omar's barn to sleep. We'll never be able to sleep out here after a scare like that."

Dannie hid a smile. Brave, bold Abie! Aloud he said, "Sure. There's fresh hay in the loft, and we can open the upper barn doors."

Yet Dannie had to admit the truth to himself: he, too, was relieved that he wouldn't need to sleep out in the woods. After all, that prowler was still out in the woods somewhere.

So, after stamping out the fire and kicking dirt over it, they headed for the farm. It wasn't until they were halfway back to the barn that the boys remembered they'd left their breakfast in the woods. But they were too tired and scared to go back, though no one admitted it. They decided to wait till morning, then go back to the hemlock woods and eat their breakfast.

Quietly the boys entered a lower barn door and went up the steps to the upper floor. The horses nickered sleepy greetings, and a few banty hens murmured in protest. Then all was quiet again.

Dannie went over to the big double doors on the *Scheierdenn* (barn floor) and flung them open for ventilation. "Just so no one walks around in his sleep, steps out here, and falls into the manure yard," he warned. "There are no steps here."

"I don't think we'll be that dumb," Seth chuckled. "But if anyone's snoring keeps us awake, we can toss him down."

The boys lined up their sleeping bags by the door openings and climbed into them, facing the outside. "This is almost like sleeping outdoors," Alva remarked. "Only we won't need to worry about being attacked by a wolf up here."

A pale sliver of a moon hung in the sky, and a million twinkling stars glittered overhead. Dannie gazed sleepily off toward the hemlock woods, listening to the familiar, peaceful nighttime sounds. The night insects were buzzing, and down in the stable he could hear the horses shuffling about in their stalls. A screech owl's wavering hoot echoing back from the hills sounded a lot less eerie from here than it had when they were in the woods.

Suddenly he sat up, peering intently off into the hemlock woods. There had been another volley of sharp barks that were suddenly cut off. Close to the trail's entrance to the woods, there appeared a pin-point of light, like the beam of a flashlight. He watched as it moved up the trail and then disappeared from sight.

Dannie shook his head. *What can it mean? If Wolf is in the woods, why did the howling stop?* The prowler might have befriended the wolf, but still, the whole thing was a mystery.

Finally, Dannie drifted off to sleep, dreaming of strange prowlers and savage beasts in the hemlock woods. Suddenly he jerked wide awake. The other boys were still sleeping soundly, but the eastern sky was alight with dawn, and the birds were beginning to sing. He wondered what it was that had startled him awake.

Then he heard it again—the far-off sound of barking from the hemlock woods. A moment later, he heard the sound of singing from the barn floor below. Omar was feeding the stock and singing the "Loblied (praise song)," unaware of the boys in the upper barn.

One by one the boys began to wake up, stretching their arms and rubbing the sleep from their eyes. Abie was the first to crawl out of his sleeping bag. "Boy, am I hungry," he announced. "Let's hope our grub is okay, and that the wolf hasn't found it. Let's go and get some pancakes started."

As the boys filed out through the barn where Omar was choring, they had to take some good-natured ribbing from him: "So, you weren't brave enough to sleep in the woods after all?" But they didn't mind and even laughed along with him at themselves. Soon they were hiking merrily on their way back to the hemlock woods.

By now, the sun was up, and the dew sparkled on the grasses and leaves. Birds sang merrily. By morning's light, the woods seemed like a different place.

Abie was the first to arrive at the campfire. He whooped with glee when he found the food untouched. Dannie heard a rustling in the thickets, quickly parted them, and found himself looking straight into the friendly hazel eyes of Wolf. With what looked like a friendly wave of his tail, Wolf wheeled around, disappeared into the brush, and headed for home, Ivor's place. He had done his duty, guarding the boy's provisions through the night!

Dannie smiled to himself and decided to say nothing to the other boys. They soon had the fire crackling as they mixed the pancake dough, ready for the frying pan.

"Looks like you get to keep your knife," Abie chuckled, as he flipped a huge pancake onto Seth's paper plate.

"And I'll have to treat each of you to an ice-cream sundae," Seth remembered. "I do have to wonder when that will ever happen. We start for home tonight, and it will probably be another five years till we visit you again."

"We won't let him forget about it, will we, Dannie?" Abie grinned. "If you don't come back to visit, Dannie and I will take a trip to Tennessee and remind you of it."

Abie was teasing and didn't know that he was really telling the truth. In a few years, he and Dannie would indeed be traveling to Tennessee together and be treated to the promised sundaes. They would reminisce about the miserable case of poison ivy the three boys had to endure after their escapade of that Saturday night.

In years to come, the boys talked often and fondly about their camping in the hemlock woods, and of the great fun they had.

6

Terror in the Dark

DANNIE immensely enjoyed his morning and evening treks through the hemlock woods while Ivor was in the hospital. Yet still, he thought wistfully of having a horse of his own to ride. He had written a letter to Daed and received a reply that when the spring work was over, he would find time to attend horse sales. Daed would be on the lookout for a good horse for Dannie.

Ivor's big gray wolf was becoming more and more companionable with Dannie. In the morning, Wolf often accompanied Dannie through the woods, as if hating to be separated from him. Then Wolf would go back to Helga alone. In the evening, Wolf would be sitting in the dell near Nancy's picnic spot, waiting for

Dannie. He would bound eagerly forward to meet Dannie when he saw him coming.

As it turned out, after Ivor's knee was replaced, some complications set in. His hospital stay lengthened into two weeks. On the fifth evening that Ivor was in the hospital, Dannie milked the old Jersey cow and tended to the other animals, as usual.

In the twilight, Helga and Dannie were sitting on the porch, having a snack of bannocks and mint tea. Wolf was stretched out full length on the porch, with his head on his paws. All of a sudden the wolf tensed and lifted his head. A low warning growl rumbled in his throat.

"Hmmmm." Helga peered anxiously into the dusk settling down in the clearing. "That means there's someone in the hemlock woods. A stranger . . . I don't know how wolf knows, but it never fails. Maybe he has a sixth sense."

Wolf got to his feet and pointed his nose to the moon. "Awa—oooh—oooh—awa—ooo!" he howled, in a drawn-out, eerie wail. Dannie shivered, even though he knew that Wolf was his friend. The sound was so spine-tingling that he couldn't help himself.

Wolf's green eyes sure could look menacing. His broad shoulders and powerful muscles were rippling under the silvery gray fur, down to the very tip of his bushy tail streaming out behind him. He looked impressive. Dannie knew they wouldn't have to fear any danger as long as Wolf was nearby.

But still, a scary feeling lingered with Dannie. *What or who was prowling in the hemlock woods?*

Suddenly Dannie remembered his conversation with Abie three days ago, when he had gone with Omar to the Shady Lane Tack Shop.

Abie had said, "My brother would like for me to take him deer spotting sometime in those hemlock woods of yours, like we four did on Saturday night. Do you think Omar would mind?"

"Of course not," Dannie had replied. "But really, you'll have to ask Ivor and Helga, who live in the long lane on the other side of the woods. Most of the hemlock woods belong to them. They have a pet wolf, and he knows whenever someone's in the woods."

Now Dannie remembered this exchange and told Helga about it. "Maybe the boys decided to go without asking for permission," he told her. "If so, Wolf's howl will probably scare them off. If you don't mind, I think I'll chain Wolf and walk out to the little cabin, and see if the boys are anywhere around."

"Well, all right, but do be careful, and don't stay too long," Helga cautioned. "I think I'll go to bed now, so be sure to turn off the lights when you come to bed. Good night."

Ivor had sent Dannie to town for a stronger chain after Wolf broke loose the night he and the other boys built their campfire. Now, after tying Wolf in the shanty with the new chain, Dannie slowly made his way along the path into the deepening woods. An uneasy feeling gripped him, and for a few moments he debated whether or not to turn back.

Clouds had blown across the face of the moon. In the woods, the night seemed as dark as pitch. But he had his flashlight. If it really was Abie out there spotting deer, he wanted to join him, so he bravely ventured on. Wolf's eerie howl and tense attitude had unnerved him somewhat, and the woods were scarier than he had remembered them to be at night.

The night insects calling and the frogs chorusing in the swamp were friendly enough. But the rustling of mice and other small creatures in the grasses and leaves made him feel jumpy. The weird "Whooo whooo whooo" of a screech owl in the tree above him didn't help matters any. For a moment he thought Wolf had gotten loose and was starting to howl. The chills chased each other up and down his spine.

When he reached the little abandoned cabin in the clearing, the beam of his flashlight showed nothing amiss. So he continued on down the side trail that passed the old dump. By this time, he thought he knew the hemlock woods by heart and had no fear of getting lost, not even in the dark.

He heard rustlings in the thickets, and the scampering of little feet in the ferny undergrowth. But as long as he wouldn't meet an irate skunk, he wouldn't mind. He stopped at the mint-overgrown spring and sat on a rock to rest, taking a refreshing drink from the tin cup Omar had hung by a wire from a low branch nearby.

The water was cold and delicious, and the warm night air was scented with the spicy odor of hemlock branches. Dannie felt himself relaxing and growing sleepy. He almost wished he were in his soft, clean bed in Helga's spare room.

All seemed as it should be in the woods. Dannie decided that if Abie had been there deer spotting, he must've left already. Suddenly the sharp crack of a twig breaking in the thickets startled him. He tensed, peering anxiously into the thickets surrounding the spring. The sound had come from behind him, in the direction of the cabin.

All seemed deathly quiet now, but an uneasy feeling came over Dannie, as if someone was close or even watching him. He shivered in the darkness, thinking that someone was crawling through the thickets. Dannie had a sudden urge to get out of there as fast as he could. He grabbed his flashlight and began to run, intending to take the roundabout way back to Ivor's place.

Suddenly he felt himself plunging down over an embankment, his arms and legs flailing wildly, his flashlight flying out of his hand and striking a rock. With a cry of terror, he turned a somersault in the air, landed on his backside, and rolled over again, straight down into the resting place of a snarling animal.

In the dark, Dannie had no way of knowing exactly what it was that sprang up, snarling ominously, while slowly retreating. Then the clouds parted so that by the light of the moon, Dannie could see fangs bared and the gleam of baleful eyes. He heard the growl of warning and saw the shaggy rising hackles.

Dannie's own hair seemed to be standing on end, too. He quickly searched in the darkness with his hand until he found a good-sized rock. Dannie was ready and aiming to throw it, but then held his shot because the beast leaped back, though still snarling viciously.

Then a low, urgent whistle sounded from somewhere behind Dannie. Immediately the savage critter slunk away and disappeared from sight. Crouching on hands and knees, Dannie fumbled around in the darkness until he found his flashlight. He pressed the button, but nothing happened. He shook it and turned the cap tighter, but it was no use. Probably the bulb was broken.

Dannie felt like crying, but he knew it wouldn't do a bit of good. He was afraid, and he didn't mind admitting it. What if there were robbers or kidnappers here in the woods? The Petersheims had taught him to pray, so pray he did, earnestly: "Our Father who art in heaven. . . . Deliver us from evil. For thine is the kingdom. Amen." It made him feel better.

7

A Night for Mulling

CRAWLING on hands and knees, Dannie made his way through the thickets, glancing nervously behind him every few minutes. He didn't know when that vicious brute would return to pounce upon him.

In a few minutes, Dannie emerged into the open and carefully surveyed the surroundings. Now the moon was out, but it still took him a few minutes to get his bearings. Suddenly he gasped. He was in a little dell, and on the ridge above him, to his left, he could see through the trees the figures of a person and a beast clearly outlined against the moonlit sky.

Dannie pulled in his breath sharply. He was sure the stranger wasn't Amish. The silhouette seemed to have a cap on backward. Dannie kept his eyes glued to the ridge, and as he watched, the two figures slowly disappeared from sight.

He shivered at the thought of an intruder skulking around in the darkness. He didn't know where the trespasser would pop up next. It all was rattling his nerves. As he waited with bated breath, not a sound broke the stillness. Then he decided to crawl away, keeping his eyes and ears open all the while, ready to flatten himself at the first sign of danger.

Dannie almost wished he had brought Wolf with him. Then he realized that things might have turned even uglier. He reckoned that Wolf could beat almost any beast, but he didn't want to see him get into a big fight. Dannie crept forward slowly and carefully, trying not to make a sound in the darkness. Every now and then, he paused, straining his senses to detect any sign of approaching danger.

He continued making his way through the undergrowth, trying to stay in the dark shadows until he was within ten feet of the creek. By now, he was close to the second waterfall, where the water cascaded down over the rocks into the pool. Since he was in a growth of tall and lush grasses, Dannie decided to stay there a while to see what would happen.

The moon was out brighter than ever, and he didn't want to risk being seen. For what seemed to be about ten minutes, he was sitting as quietly as he could, keeping his senses alert all the while. He heard a cautious movement to the left of him, in the direction of the creek.

Dannie peered into the darkness, trying to see

where the noise came from and what it was. The mysterious thing was staying in the shadows of the thickets. A moment later, he heard the faintest trace of a splash in the creek. Dannie crouched low, trembling with fear and suspense. He thought he detected a movement in the bushes and kept his eyes glued to where the motion had been, his heart thumping with fear.

In the distance, a great horned owl was calling "Whoo whoo whoo," and he wondered if it really was an owl or perhaps some secret signal. A fish jumped up out of the water in the pool and slapped back down with a splash that startled him badly.

Here and there, shafts of moonlight penetrated the branches overhead, but at times more clouds were blowing across the face of the moon. Every now and then, the night seemed to become dark as pitch, adding suspense to the eerie scene.

Then he heard another cautious movement, this time on the other side of the creek, and more splashes. Some clouds finished passing over the moon, and for a minute it was not so dark.

As Dannie was straining his eyes to see through the gloom, he thought he could make out the outline of the beast going through the creek and emerging on the other side. For a moment he could again see the silhouette of the stranger, who quickly crouched low and crept into the shadows.

Dannie heard a grating sound, as if a rock were slowly and stealthily being moved around, then all was quiet again. He waited for another fifteen or twenty minutes. Hearing and seeing nothing more, he stealthily made his way back to Helga's place, moving as fast as he could without making much noise.

With a sigh of great thankfulness, he finally reached the clearing. He checked on all the animals before going to bed. When he reached Wolf, he patted him on the head, then took off his shoes, snapped off the lights, and crept up the stairs to his bed. He decided to say nothing about his adventures to Helga in the morning. It would only frighten her, and she would be safe with Wolf here, anyhow.

Tossing and turning on the bed, Dannie found himself still too tense and wound up to sleep. He didn't know what to make of the weird goings-on in the hemlock woods, as he mulled over them. Finally he resolved to put it all out of his mind and quit thinking about it.

The next thing he knew, he was waking up, and the rising sun was casting its rays through his window. The big old grandfather's clock in the hall downstairs was bonging six times. Dannie sprang out of bed, knowing he had overslept. He dressed quickly, sniffing the delicious aroma of frying bacon that was drifting up the stairs.

"Good morning," Helga greeted him cheerily as she poured glasses of orange juice, then set a plate of freshly baked biscuits and plum jam on the table. "I decided to let you sleep a while longer. You've been up so early every morning."

Usually Dannie tended the animals before Helga had breakfast ready, but this morning he ate first.

"I'm sorry I overslept," Dannie apologized. "Next I'll have to get myself an alarm clock."

"Don't worry about it," Helga brushed his apology aside. "Why, oversleeping once saved Ivor's great-grandfather's life. During the time he ordinarily would've been out milking the cow, a twister went through, demolished the barn, and killed the cow."

This put Helga into a storytelling mood. Dannie found out that she was nearly as good a storyteller as Ivor. She enjoyed having an audience just as much as her husband.

"Yes, he had quite an adventuresome life," Helga continued between bites of biscuits and plum jam. "His name was Jedediah Winters, and he was a frontier parson, a circuit rider. He was sent to try to make peace between the settlers and the Indians, a friendly tribe in that area.

"Jed tried to reason with scoundrels cheating the Indians and giving them strong drink. He must've been brave and fearless. Like Daniel Boone, he managed to get himself into all kinds of scrapes and out of them again."

She launched into the story and forgot herself. Though Dannie loved to listen to it, he found himself glancing at the clock. He needed to do the chores and get back to helping Omar. But he knew Helga was lonely while Ivor was away, with no one but Wolf to talk to. His job now was to relax and listen.

Helga saw Dannie eyeing the clock once and jumped up from the table. "I'm sorry," she said, "for holding you here when you're already running late. I'll finish my story some other time. You just go ahead and tend to those animals."

"Well, all right," Dannie agreed, "but I do want to hear more of Jed's adventures sometime, so don't forget. I'm going to leave Wolf chained this morning, so he'll be with you today."

Without giving an explanation, Dannie hurried out the door to feed the animals.

8

Silly or Nice?

NANCY carefully scrubbed down the floor of the calf barn and mixing room with the high-pressure hose. Then she took off her chore boots and apron, hung the apron on a hook outside the door, and stepped outside. Mornings were her favorite part of the day, and she wished she'd have the time to take a long, leisurely stroll.

Dew sparkled on the grass, the air was fresh and fragrant, and the purple martins seemed to be bubbling over as they gave vocal notice of the joy of the morning. From the rosebush, robins sang with happy abandon. Other birds she couldn't name added their music to nature's choir.

The pond lay shimmering and inviting in the distance, with morning mists rising up from it. For a few minutes, Nancy half envied the cow as she peacefully ambled her way down to the meadow, with its misty buttercups and forget-me-nots. Lush grasses and wildflowers, warm breezes and floating mists brought the heady delights of springtime to all the senses.

This morning was no time to dawdle. Nancy had promised her sister Mary that she would go today and help her catch up with the spring work. But first Nancy wanted to make a batch of oatmeal cookies to take along. She would also gather a big bunch of meadow tea, which Mary liked better than the peppermint growing in her garden tea bed.

Omar was soon in for breakfast. Nancy filled their cups with steaming, flavorful tea. She put the platter of ham and eggs in the middle of the table, beside the pot of still-bubbling oatmeal on a potholder.

When she reached into the cupboard for the sugar bowl, a fat envelope pack fell to the counter. "Oh, there's the girls' circle letter. I haven't answered yet," she moaned. "When will I ever find the time to do that? Do you want to read it, Omar, before I send it on its merry way?"

Omar shook his head. "Nope, not if it's the one your girlfriends from back home started. It wouldn't be any good if Sally's not in it."

Nancy had to smile. "Of course, you wouldn't think so. But it *is* interesting to me."

After they had bowed their heads for silent grace, Nancy proceeded to tell Omar some of the more interesting parts of the circle letter.

One girl wrote that on her first date, when they came back to her home from the singing, she struck a match to light the lamp. Because she was feeling a bit rattled, she laid the still-hot match on the ruffle of her bonnet. Soon it burst into flame! Her beau grabbed the bonnet and ran outside with it. By the time he put out the fire, the ruffle was neatly burned off!

Another reported that her brother bought a birthday gift for his longtime *Aldi* (girlfriend), gift wrapped it himself, and hid it in his wardrobe. He was planning to give it to her the next Sunday evening. When this letter writer was cleaning her brother's room, she found the package and couldn't resist playing a prank on him.

She unwrapped the package and put a baby's pacifier inside with the silverware he was giving, and carefully rewrapped the gift. That sister wrote, "I would've given a pretty penny to see both their faces when she opened the gift!"

"*Unvergleichlich!* (strange). What a low-down trick." Omar was aghast. "If sisters do things like that, I'd better be careful."

Nancy shook her head. "Don't worry. He had asked for it. His sister owed him one, and to my way of thinking, he had it coming to him.

"A few weeks earlier, she had set up the stepladder to the porch roof and was washing a high hall window that couldn't be opened from the inside or the outside. Seeing her up there, her brother had sneaked off with the stepladder, then went to the neighbors to run an errand, intending to be right back and let her down.

"He stayed to help the neighbor bale hay and forgot all about his sister on the roof. Since she lived in a long lane and was at home alone, she was stranded up there, hopping mad, all afternoon. Finally their bachelor neighbor drove in the lane, wanting to borrow something, and gallantly came to her rescue, much to her chagrin and humiliation!"

Nancy couldn't help but laugh again as Omar snorted with mirth. She went on, "One of the girls in the next letter teased her by asking whether it's true that he got her to agree to go with him on a date before he helped her down. I can hardly wait to see her reply the next time the package comes around."

"They must be a lively bunch," Omar had to admit. "Just make sure you don't write anything about me or Andrew in your letters."

"No fear of that," Nancy assured him. "There wouldn't be anything silly to write about you even if I'd want to."

When the cookies were baked, Nancy started walking down the lane, heading for Mary and Jacob's place. She was looking forward to a day of visiting with her big sister and enjoying the children. Her thoughts returned to what she'd told Omar, that there wouldn't be anything silly to write about him.

"I should have said, 'And neither about Andrew,'" she told herself. "He used to be a great one to play pranks and tease. But not anymore. Now he seems quite manly, and I can't help but admire him for it."

A rattle of gravel from behind startled her, interrupting her thoughts, and she quickly turned to see what it was. "Andrew," she nearly gasped. Before she could stop herself she blurted out, "I was just thinking about you."

"So?" He smiled as he kept pace beside her on his scooter. "Good or bad?"

Nancy blushed. "Um . . . nothing bad." Seeing his twinkling eyes, she relaxed.

"I'm on my way over to Jacob's for the day. She needs some help with her spring work."

"And I'm going there, too, to repair a harness. Too bad I don't have my new horse yet, or I could take you over in style."

"That would be nice," Nancy admitted, and then she couldn't think of anything more to say. Andrew, too, was silent for a while, as if wanting to say something, but not quite having the courage for it. By the roadside, a rabbit scuttled out from under a clump of clover and disappeared into the underbrush.

"That reminds me," Andrew spoke up. "Little sister Sarah had a disappointment this morning when she went to feed her bunnies. Two of them were killed and carried off. Some thievin' varmint must've been awfully desperate for a meal. We haven't had trouble of that sort for years, and we're not all that close to the woods."

"That's too bad," Nancy said sympathetically. "Ivor's Wolf chases rabbits in the wild, but I'm sure he wouldn't have done something like that."

"No, he's too well-trained for that. But it could've been a stray dog."

They had reached Jacobs' place now, and Andrew

headed for the barn. "See you on Sunday night at the singing," he called after Nancy.

Warm circles chased each other around Nancy's heart as she made her way to the house. Andrew sure was nice.

9

The Storm

RETURNING home from Helga's place through the hemlock woods, Dannie found everything peaceful, with no sign of last night's adventure. If he had not been running late, he'd have taken the time to go the long way round, to inspect the area around the waterfall. That was where he'd seen the shadowy figures of the stranger and beast disappear.

The woods were so peaceful and delightful, dappled with sunshine, sparkling with dew, and ringing with the chorus of birdsong. He chided himself for being afraid the night before. "Why, maybe it was only a boy from the village out for a moonlight stroll with his dog," he muttered.

Dannie laughed at himself for making a mountain

out of a molehill. He decided to say nothing to Omar and Nancy about it.

On the farm, it was another busy day of making hay. There were signs of an approaching storm in the afternoon, so they hurried to finish before the rain arrived. That storm passed off to the north. But in the evening while they were doing the chores, another one was approaching, with rumbles of thunder in the northwest sky.

By the time the veal calves were fed and Dannie was ready to head over to Helga's place, the wind was rising. Jagged streaks of lightning zipped from the clouds to the earth. Flocks of barn swallows circled the barn in zigzag flight, nervous about the approaching storm.

Dannie decided that he could probably make it over to Helga's before the storm descended in earnest. Big thunderheads were piling up above the west end of the hemlock woods, and the gusts were stirring up small whirlpool eddies of dust in the field. Dannie hurried, half running up the path. He had no desire to be struck by lightning or drenched to the skin.

"Now if only I'd have my horse, I could be there in short order," he griped to himself. The thunder rumbling in the distance was becoming louder, and the lightning silhouetted the ragged white edges of the thunderheads. By the time Dannie reached the first spring pool, the crashes of thunder seemed too close. He realized he wasn't going to make it to Helga's before the storm hit.

The spectacle of jagged lightning was awesome and fearful. A big drop of water plopped down on

Dannie's head, soon followed by more and more of them. As the skies opened and a regular downpour hit, he ran for the shelter of the little cabin in the clearing. The rain beat down on the roof of the cabin in earnest. Peals of thunder seemed to shake its very walls before reverberating off the hills.

When a flame of sheet lightning suddenly lit up the whole room, something in the corner caught Dannie's eye. He directed the beam of his new flashlight toward it and saw a bag of dog food and a short red leash with a clip on the end. Dannie's attention was again drawn to the window when another vivid streak of lightning lit up the landscape, momentarily outlining the trees with awesome clarity and splendor.

Then with a mighty roar and crash, a big tree blew over and toppled to the ground close to the cabin. Dannie shuddered at the violent display of the power of nature, wondering if next the cabin would be lifted from its foundation. Suddenly the sound of the descending torrents of rain began to change to plink! crackle! plop! "Hailstones," Dannie exclaimed aloud.

The hail lasted for only a minute or two. Immediately after it ended, the storm began to abate. The rumblings of thunder steadily decreased until only a few sullen mutterings were heard anymore. Dannie ventured out for Helga's place, detouring around the fallen branches and debris on the path.

When he reached the porch, Helga was seated there on the old hickory rocker, with Wolf stretched out at her side, awaiting him. She greeted him with genuine gladness. "My, that was quite a storm, and I was afraid you would be caught in the middle of it. It caused a heap of damage. The big old oak tree near the cow stable crashed and downed the fence!

"As soon as the storm was over, I went out, and Bessie the cow was nowhere to be seen. Her tracks lead into the hemlock woods. I sure hope you can find her and bring her back before it gets too dark and she wanders too far. I just wish Ivor would be here," she said anxiously. "Nothing like this ever happened here before this."

Dannie did his best to reassure the old lady: "Don't worry about it. I know my way through the woods, and I'll bring the cow back as fast as I can. I'll take Wolf along. With him leading the way, bringing the cow back shouldn't be hard."

As he headed toward the woods, he called, "C'mon Wolf, let's go."

The big gray animal needed no further invitation. He sprang to Dannie's side, eager to go for a jaunt. Following the cow's tracks was easy at first, but as the woods deepened and the dusky twilight descended, Dannie had to rely more and more on Wolf's prowess.

"I can't see how she wandered this far already," Dannie grumbled. "She must've been badly frightened, and hoofing it mighty fast."

Every now and then, he and Wolf had to detour around fallen branches and muddy washouts. The trail led into the waterfall area. In the deepening dusk, Dannie again had an uneasy feeling of being watched. A low growl from Wolf added to his suspicions. Wolf was sniffing the ground near the bank of the creek where he had seen the shadowy figures disappear the other night.

Dannie snapped on his flashlight and plainly saw the imprint of a shoe alongside some paw prints. He compared the tracks with his own and Wolf's, and saw that they weren't the same. Wolf's paw prints were much bigger than those paw prints, and the tread on the sole of Dannie's shoes was different from the imprints he saw. "Let's follow these tracks, Wolf," Dannie said excitedly. "With you along—"

He stopped short as a low growl sounded from just ahead. Wolf answered with an even more ominous and menacing growl, then threw back his head and howled, "Awa-oooh—oooh—awa—oooo!" The eerie spine-tingling sound reverberated back from the hills.

Dannie felt that this surely would be fair warning to the intruders to get out of there fast. He shone his flashlight into the bushes ahead and thought he saw a movement. Venturing closer, he gasped aloud. It was a movement—a big rock was teetering from side to side! One end of it was pivoting against an embankment. There were scuffling noises, and then the movements stopped, and all was quiet.

Wolf tensed, as if ready to spring, but Dannie quickly stopped him with a restraining hand on his shoulder. Something told him that it wouldn't be wise to press further. Besides, there was the cow to find and return to her pen. "Let's go, Wolf," he said in a low voice. "We can come back later."

He was suddenly immensely relieved to be leaving the area. There was a sinister feeling here that he didn't like. He even had an urge to run, but contented himself with a fast walk. Five minutes later, he and Wolf came upon old Bessie, contentedly chewing her cud near the old dump. Getting her started on the homeward path was a breeze.

Before long, Dannie and Wolf were herding Bessie into her stable. Helga came out of the house with a hammer and nails and told Dannie, "Just nail two boards over the stable entrance for now. It's too dark and too late to fix the barnyard fence tonight."

Helga was in much better spirits now that the cow was safely home. After Dannie milked the cow and finished the other chores, she had a snack laid out for him on the porch.

10

A Varmint Attack

HELGA'S ice cold mint tea was delicious. The little fruit-filled cakes she served were almost as good as Nancy's half-moon pies, Dannie thought. He was relaxing in the old hickory rocker on the porch, with Wolf at his feet and his muzzle resting on his knee. Ivor's old tomcat was back, sitting on the porch railing with his tail curled around him and his eyes closed. He had a habit of disappearing for weeks at a time, but he always came back.

They chatted about the storm and the farmwork, but Dannie decided not to bother Helga by saying anything about the intruders in the hemlock woods. "It's story time," he reminded Helga. "I've been wondering all day about the adventures of old Jedediah, the circuit rider." He caressed the silky head on his knee.

Helga smiled, pleased that Dannie was interested and had remembered. "I was just thinking today that maybe I'd better wait till Ivor gets home and let him finish the tale. He's a born storyteller and loves the chance to have someone listen to him.

"I was in to visit Ivor today, and he's simply pining away to be able to come home." Her face brightened. "He's getting better, though, and that means a lot. He—"

Helga suddenly stopped and held up a hand for silence. From far off in the hemlock hills came a series of sharp, yelping barks and growls. Dannie shivered, remembering how he had plunged down over an embankment and nearly into the snarling fangs of a vicious beast.

Now that he was thinking of it, he did not recall ever seeing a bank right there, even though he had explored the woods a lot in years past. He resolved to investigate the area and see what was going on. But he said nothing to Helga about his decision.

When silence again echoed back from the hills, Helga spoke: "Wolf and I keep hearing that from time to time, in the woods. There's something uncanny going on over there, and I wish I knew what it was. Look at Wolf now."

Their shaggy friend had risen up, and his whole body was tensed. His nose pointed toward the area from which the barking sounds had come. Dannie laid a hand on Wolf's shoulder. He had no desire to hear that eerie howl just now. In a few minutes, Wolf relaxed and lay down on the porch again.

"Wolf's been doing more howling lately than he usually does." Helga sounded worried. "Maybe it's mostly because Ivor isn't here. But I still think there's a mystery over there in the woods. Do be careful when you travel back and forth in the morning and evening."

Later, as Dannie was lying in bed and thinking over the day's happenings, he certainly had to agree with Helga. There was a mystery in the woods, and he was determined to find out what it was, and soon.

He drifted off to sleep. Sometime later, he was awakened by a ferocious racket, the terrified bleating of sheep, and Wolf's fierce howls and growls. In a flash he was out of bed and jumping into his pants. He grabbed a flashlight and dashed down the stairs.

Helga was already in the kitchen, in a long white nightgown, with her hair disheveled and her eyes big and scared. "Wh—what could it be?" she sputtered. "Please be careful. Oh, if only Ivor were here."

"I will," Dannie flung back as he dived for the door. The din in the shanty where Wolf was chained was deafening, but Dannie headed for the barn first. The sight that greeted him in the corral sickened him. There lay a spring lamb, with its throat torn open, covered with blood.

The three mother sheep with their other offspring were huddled in a corner, piteously bleating. In the mud close to the carcass were the footprints of the culprit, and on the lowest rung of the barbed-wire fence clung a tuft of tawny fur.

Dannie felt sick as he viewed the dead lamb. "If Wolf would've been loose," he muttered, "this wouldn't have happened."

Helga came pattering out to the barnyard in her slippers, carrying a lantern. Her eyes showed horror at the sight, but there wasn't much to say. She stood gazing dejectedly at the lamb and finally said, "Pen the sheep in the barn, Dannie, and come back to bed. In all the years we've lived here, it has never before been necessary to do that, but there's something sinister in the hemlock woods, I'm afraid.

"That lamb was my pet, the one I bottle-fed, but it just wouldn't grow for me." Choking back a sob, she headed for the house.

Dannie went into the shanty to calm Wolf. "There, old boy," he said soothingly, although he felt like he needed to be comforted himself. "After this I'll chain you outside the barn, and then we'll see if any varmints come trespassing."

He almost took the shovel from the corner to bury the lamb, then thought better of it. He would ask Omar to look at it first.

Back in the kitchen, Helga had made some tea. She offered Dannie a cup of it. "Tomorrow we'll decide what must be done," she declared. "Tell Omar to come over, if possible. Also bring Andrew Fisher, if he can come. We need some men with guns to track the critter. I'll phone the game commission and report this. I'm sure they'll consent to let us hunt it down."

Dannie nodded. He felt good about letting older, wiser shoulders carry the responsibility.

"I don't know why all this has to happen just when Ivor isn't here," Helga went on. "He'd know just what to do. Yes, well, it's time to get back to bed. I'll try to forget about it and get some sleep, and you do the same."

The next morning when Dannie was walking home through the hemlock woods, all seemed peaceful again. The birds were singing as if there wasn't a care in the world, and the squirrels were as happy and busy as ever. The sun shone brightly, bringing out the spicy, piney scent of the trees.

He had thought it best to leave Wolf with Helga, but he missed his company. On the way, he detoured toward the old dump so he could check out the area where he'd fallen down over the embankment. Seeing it reminded Dannie of Bandit, his pet raccoon, how he was fascinated with shiny objects he picked out of the dump. He felt a twinge of homesickness for his old pet. Maybe someday he'd have another one.

By the old stump stood a rusty old iron porch chair that he hadn't noticed before. Dannie carefully studied the ground nearby. There were tracks all around the chair, tracks of shoes smaller than his own, along with large dog tracks. Those shoe tracks puzzled him. They were shaped more daintily, like girls' shoes. He couldn't figure it out.

Traveling on down the path, he came to the embankment that hadn't been there before, and he gave a low whistle of amazement. Someone had built a rock wall here and dug out for a pool beneath it. Water slowly trickled into it from that spring that bubbled up out of the rocks. The spring's flow had recently been diverted this way, and Dannie couldn't help but admire the neat job that had been done.

"All it needs is a bed of mint around it yet," he said aloud. But who could have done it? He was sure it wasn't Nancy or Sally, for he had just yesterday heard Nancy say that she and Sally hadn't been back here for ages. They told each other that they wanted to come to the woods as soon as an opportunity arose.

There were tracks around the spring, too, but they appeared to be slightly larger than the dainty shoe tracks, more like boot tracks.

"It all beats me," Dannie muttered as he trudged back to the dump. "I wish we could solve the mystery going on in these hemlock woods. I think I'll search the little cabin yet before I leave."

The heavy old door with its iron clasp creaked as Dannie pushed it open. The first thing that caught his eye was a piece of driftwood on the mantle, entwined with green vining ivy. It was planted in an old flowerpot and had recently been watered. The cabin had been freshly swept, and the windows were clean.

Dannie looked around the cabin carefully for the bag of dog food and the leash that had been there the night before, during the storm. But the cabin was bare.

"Ya, well, whoever put it there, took it away again," he told himself. "I'll have to hurry back to help Omar now. But I sure hope we can figure things out soon."

11

The Woodland Stroll

NANCY hurriedly gathered up the throw rugs from the kitchen floor and spread them out on the porch. Then she grabbed the broom and vigorously swept them, making the dust fly.

These rugs held precious memories for her. *Mammi* (Grandma) Petersheim had crocheted them and given them as a housewarming gift for her and Omar. They were in various shades of lavender, purple, blue, and black—each one different—and made from outgrown shirts and dresses the family had once worn.

Nancy's eager anticipation of the day's plans lent wings to her feet. There was the cleaning to finish, some early strawberries to pick, and pies to bake. Then this afternoon, Sally was coming over. They were taking time off to walk over to Helga's and to enjoy the hemlock woods, something they had been planning to do for quite awhile.

It had never seemed to suit one or the other of them on a Sunday. Omar and Dannie were taking part of the day off to go to a horse sale with Andrew, giving the girls the idea that they could take time off, too. They wanted to carry strawberries over to Helga and help her get them ready for the freezer. Then for tonight, Helga had invited them all to go along with her to the hospital to visit Ivor.

So Nancy worked busily and happily, sweeping and scrubbing the floors, shining the windows and the old black cookstove, which was easy to polish to a gleam now that it had no fire in it.

Next she mixed pie dough, deftly rolling it out and fitting it into the pie pans. She would cook some raisin filling for Omar's favorite kind of pie, and also make seven strawberry pies, which Dannie thought were too good to be real. Nancy chuckled as she remembered how his eyes had lit up when she told him she was planning to make strawberry pies.

Dannie had also been so enthused about attending that horse sale and helping Andrew pick out a new buggy horse. Thus far, Andrew had been driving his buggy with his dad's horse, but now it was time for a horse of his own.

Secretly, Dannie was also planning to pick out a riding horse for himself and see if he could persuade Omar to buy it for him. Then Daed wouldn't have to bother getting him one.

When dinnertime came, Nancy was glad she didn't have to take the time to cook. She was the only one home and could just fix herself a cheese-and-lettuce sandwich and some chocolate milk. There were a lot of baking dishes to wash. She was just flinging the dishwater out the door when she spied Sally traipsing in the lane.

"Ready to go?" she called cheerily at the door. "This will seem like old times."

"Just about," Nancy replied. "I hope you'll help me carry these strawberries, and I think I'll take a raisin pie for Helga, too."

"I have a bouquet of lily of the valley for her," Sally said. "She told me once that it's her favorite flower."

The girls were soon on their way, each carrying a basket and enjoying the beautiful day. At the entrance to the hemlock woods, they stopped, as they always did, and took deep breaths of the spicy, sun-drenched scent. They almost swooned as they gazed up into the enormous trees overhead.

Nancy spied a pair of squirrels frisking from branch to branch, as breezes whispered through the sweeping green branches. "These woods must be the loveliest spot on earth," she declared, "especially in springtime."

From its perch in the lofty branches above, a cardinal called, "Good cheer, good cheer, good cheer."

"There goes a chipmunk," Sally pointed to the tiny striped creature darting into the ferny underbrush.

"I can hardly wait until we reach the spring. Thinking of that clear, sparkling mint-flavored water makes me thirsty already."

"Me too," Nancy agreed. "It's just around the next bend. I can hear the trickle of water already. Let's stop there for a while and drink in the water and the beauty of our surroundings."

"And rest!" Sally sighed as she sank down onto a rock by the little pool and set down her basket. "I've walked twice as far as you have."

"Let me get you a drink of water." Nancy reached for the tin cup that Omar had hung onto a long wire suspended from a tree branch, so no curious coon would carry it off. The mint bed lent its inviting fragrance to the air. She pinched off a choice sprig.

"I wish there'd be a spring like this in our backyard," she told Sally dreamily. "I'd like to build another little pool there, surround it with rocks, and have the spring water trickling down over rocks like a waterfall. Then I'd have little goldfish in it instead of minnows. But the trouble is, I'd be building it for you."

"That would suit me fine." Sally smiled, deepening her dimples, and added teasingly, "I think I know where I could build one for you, too."

Nancy pretended not to hear and changed the subject. "See that gorgeous butterfly hovering over the mint bed?"

Just then a bumblebee came buzzing by and landed on Sally's arm. "Oooh!" she shrieked, jumping to her feet and wildly waving her arms, to shake off the bee.

At the same moment, the rock supporting Sally wobbled. She lost her balance, and her feet slipped into the pool with a splash. Nancy quickly reached a hand out to her, and Sally grasped it so frantically that she pulled Nancy off her rock, too. They both stumbled into the shallow pool.

Laughing merrily, the girls helped each other out onto solid ground and tried to wring out the bottom of their wet skirts.

"I wish Omar could see you with that daub of mud on the tip of your nose," Nancy giggled.

"Hmmph," Sally snorted, scooping up fresh water out of the flow to wash it off. "My nose is upturned enough the way it is."

"This is just like old times," Nancy said wistfully, thinking of the fun the girls had together before Omar and Sally were dating. She half wished that things could always be the way they had been then. But she knew that they couldn't be carefree girls forever. Sometime they'd have to start being proper women.

"Let's hope these skirts dry before we reach Helga's place." Sally wrung out a few more drops. "I guess we have a good excuse now, to explore as long as we want to, while they dry."

As the girls went strolling on their merry way, they were unaware that they were being watched. Someone hidden in a woodland dell, inside a shelter made of hemlock branches and fronds, was wistfully looking at the girls, envying their friendship and merry chatter, and longing for someone to talk to.

"Let's stop at the little cabin," Nancy was saying. "We never did get done what we planned long ago, to clean it properly and sleep out in the cabin sometime."

"I wouldn't want to now anymore," Sally said with

a shudder. "Not with a wild beast around like the one that killed Helga's poor innocent lamb. It's hard to believe that anything that savage could be in these peaceful woods."

"Maybe it's not here anymore. Perhaps it's miles away by now," Nancy suggested. "You know, Omar and Andrew spent a half day in these woods with their guns, trying to track it down, and got nary a glimpse of it."

"I sure hope it's gone!" Sally said fervently. "I wish I hadn't happened to think of it. Now it's starting to give me the creeps. I don't think I want to explore much after all."

At that moment the woods reverberated with the eerie, haunting wail "Awa-oooh-oooh-awa-oooo" of Ivor's Wolf, echoing through the pines.

"*Ach, mei* (oh, my), let's head straight for Helga's place, wet skirts or not," Sally urged. "I think I'd rather listen to one of her stories than explore after all."

"Suits me fine," Nancy agreed. "There are these berries to prepare for the freezer, and we'll have to walk back yet." But secretly she wished Sally hadn't happened to think of that lamb, at least until they'd explored the old cabin and the dump.

12

Lost in the Woods

THE girls were sitting in Helga's kitchen, cool because it was shaded by the giant hemlocks. They had bowls in their laps and were capping strawberries. Their talk centered on the dead lamb, discussing what beast might have killed it.

"You know what it reminds me of?" Helga asked. "When I was a child, we lived on the edge of a wilderness, and a few panthers were still around. As soon as I saw that poor lamb killed, it reminded me of the work of a panther."

"But there aren't any panthers in the hemlock woods," Nancy reminded her. "At least we haven't heard any panthers scream."

Helga nodded. "Well, when my sister and I were

little girls, we were lost in the woods once. We heard a panther scream and were terribly frightened. Did I ever tell you that story?"

"I think you told us about it several years ago, but maybe not the whole story. I'd love to hear it," Sally answered, popping a strawberry into her mouth.

"Me too," Nancy agreed enthusiastically. "I love thrilling stories, as long as there's a good ending. I know you were rescued or you wouldn't be here today to tell it."

"It was a close call, though. We were having a tea party near the woods, using a big flat rock for a table. We set our dolls around it and used bark for our dishes, acorn cups for cups, and twigs for tableware. Then we wanted moss for our tablecloth."

Helga paused, thinking about that day long ago. "As we looked for moss nearby, my little sister saw a pretty hummingbird and dashed after it. But it kept flying just out of reach. Then we spied a lovely butterfly on a wildflower, and both of us wanted to catch that.

"The flying critters lured us into the woods, where we found lots of moss." Helga chuckled as she remembered. "We found a creek and were wading and splashing in it. When we started for home, we climbed out and headed the wrong way."

Helga stopped to eat a strawberry. "I think it would've killed my mother if we had perished there in the woods. Our family had five children, but three had already died of typhoid fever. We two girls were all she had left."

"What happened next?" Sally asked eagerly as she helped herself to another berry.

"We walked to a berry patch, but the bushes were stripped of berries. When we saw big animal tracks there, we knew danger was close. A twig snapped behind us. We whirled around, face to face with a mother brown bear and her two little cubs.

"When the big bear lowered to all fours, we ran. Behind us, we heard the bear huffing and crashing through underbrush for a while. Finally we found a big hollow log, crawled into the open end, and pulled leaves in after us.

"As we cried in the hiding place, we heard timber wolves howling, small animals stirring nearby, and an owl hooting, 'Whooo, whooo, whoo.' When nearly asleep we were awakened by a terrible scream. Whew!"

Helga passed a hand over her forehead, reliving the awful feeling. "We prayed. God must've sent a guardian angel to care for us, because the creature didn't come any closer. Once we heard a snuffling sound—perhaps a bear hunting for mice or insects around the log. Providence spared us."

The storyteller got up for the potato masher, to crush her bowl of berries for supper. The girls were so absorbed in the story that they had nearly forgotten to keep their hands busy capping berries.

"Do keep on," Nancy urged. "How your poor mother must've worried, knowing her little darlings were at the mercy of wild beasts."

Helga nodded. "Ivor and I never had children of

our own, but I can imagine how awful it was for our parents. They spent all night hunting for us. We fell asleep in the log. When we awoke and crawled out, the sun was shining and birds were singing. We started off, again heading the wrong way.

"We found a few more berries to eat, but by afternoon we were tired, hungry, and discouraged. We lay down under a crab apple tree to rest.

"Later we snacked at another patch of berries and drank from a stream. As evening shadows lengthened, we climbed a ridge and took refuge in a small cave. We were likely in a big cat's lair, what with the chewed-up bones, fur, and a strong animal smell. Soon we heard another spine-tingling, horrible scream. It must have been a panther.

"We screamed back, not knowing if we would be eaten alive. About that time, Dad and a few neighbors found a piece of torn dress caught on a thorn bush. A bit further, they found another piece of our clothing and began to call for us.

"Then they heard a faint cry from up in the rocks and quickly rode their horses up. They found us and hugged us, laughing and crying at the same time. Oh, what glorious relief!

"They sat us up on the horses, in front of the men. In a short time we were home with our mother."

Helga rose and went to the cupboard to find freezer boxes for the berries. "I almost forgot that tonight's the evening we all go to visit Ivor. Dannie will be here early, and I want to help him with the chores so we can get an early start."

Nancy jumped up, too, and glanced at the clock. "And we have to get back to make an early start in the calf barn, too. Thanks for the interesting afternoon."

Reaching into her basket, Nancy took out the raisin pie and presented it to Helga with a flourish. Helga already had Sally's bouquet of flowers in a vase on the windowsill.

"You girls are so good to me," Helga said, with tears in her eyes. "I simply don't know what I'd do without you people. How can I ever repay you?"

"You already have," Sally spoke up, "just with your friendship and kindness."

"And by offering to take us along to visit Ivor," Nancy reminded her. "Now we won't need to hire a driver."

They waved to her and quickly set out through the hemlock woods.

13

A Hospital Visit

WHEN Helga came driving in Omar's lane, in her old but well-cared-for car, Sally and Andrew were already in the backseat. Omar, Dannie, and Nancy had hurried as much as they could with the chores. But even so, Nancy still had her *Kapp* (cap/covering) to pin on and tie, and her shoes were still in the closet.

Dannie had been so excited about the horse Andrew bought that it was all he could talk about during supper. He was still at it when they got into the car. "Did the new horse come already?" he asked Andrew.

"Sure did! He's tied in our stall now. The former owner brought him over in his horse trailer."

"Isn't he a beaut!" Dannie said enthusiastically. "It was the one I had picked out for myself."

"He was one glum boy," Omar told Helga, "when I told him I wouldn't be able to afford a horse like that. But he sure chirked up when Andrew bought the horse and told Dannie he could use him to ride over to your place and back every evening and morning."

"How nice of him," Helga smiled at Andrew. "I wish I'd be able to buy him for Dannie, but with these hospital expenses. . . ."

"I'm afraid Andrew would be the glum boy then," Sally said, laughing. "This way everyone can be happy."

"What kind and color of horse is he?" Helga wondered. "Black, like Omar's Beauty?"

"Oh no," Dannie glowed with happiness. "He's golden, and he even has a light-gold or ivory-colored tail and mane. I always wanted a horse like that."

"Sounds like a palomino." Helga guided the car onto the main highway and merged into traffic.

Andrew nodded. "But he wasn't half as expensive as Omar thought he'd be. I guess I was lucky. Maybe most of our people would rather not drive a horse of that color. Did you think of a name for him yet, Dannie? He doesn't have any papers."

Dannie was quiet for a few moments. "I had thought of naming him Silas. I-I once had a crow by that name. But really, he's your horse."

"Silas it shall be then," Andrew said good-naturedly. "Silas or Midas or whatever."

"You boys can call him what you wish, but I'm going to call him Silky," Sally put in. "That's almost like Silas, and he's got a silky tail and mane."

"Very well," Dannie agreed. "Let's name him Silky Silas."

What with the lively conversation in the car, in no time at all, it seemed, they had reached the city streets and then the hospital grounds. Helga led the way through the halls and into an elevator.

They stepped out on the third floor, and from there it was only a few steps to Ivor's room. Helga went in first. The others remained outside the doorway, but Ivor's booming voice calling, "Come in, come in!" ushered them inside.

"Where's my Dannie boy?" Ivor's face and eyes crinkled into a big smile as he extended his hand. "They tell me you're doing a good job of tending my animals."

Dannie was about to tell about the lamb being killed by a varmint. Just in time, he remembered that Helga had asked him not to mention it. There was no need for Ivor to know such sad news until he had recovered further and was home.

Ivor was greeting the others just as heartily as he had greeted Dannie. He was glad for his visitors and didn't seem sick at all, except for being slightly pale instead of his usual ruddy color.

"I'm just living for the day when I can go home and have a drink of fresh pure spring water, along with a taste of mint. This chlorinated city water—bah!" Ivor made a face. "If it wouldn't be for the ice in it, I wouldn't dare to taste it."

Ivor entertained his visitors instead of vice versa. "This is the second time I'm in the hospital," he told them. "The first time was when I was just a lad. I was visiting my uncle in the West, and we decided to take a jaunt up into the hills on horseback. We took our bedrolls along and slept out under the stars.

"That night we banked our campfire so it would be easy for us to stir it up in the morning for cooking our breakfast. The air was mighty pure and bracing up there, and I slept like a log.

"Sometime in the night, I awoke with a start, sensing danger nearby. I couldn't figure out what it was. The night seemed quiet and peaceful enough, with wind sighing through the evergreens, and a pair of whippoorwills calling to each other.

"Did you ever hear whippoorwills?" When Dannie shook his head no, Ivor pursed his lips and imitated one. "They have a plaintive tone, and the mate kept on courteously answering back. I can remember it all plain as day.

"Wolves were howling in the distance, but that wasn't what made me uneasy. I threw a bit of kindling on the last glowing embers of the fire. When it flared up, I saw a faint glittering in the dark. It slowly crept across the ground. When it made a writhing movement, closer to the fire, I saw it was a huge rattlesnake!

"The rattler was slithering past the fire, its scales glittering in the firelight, right toward us. Knowing that such a deadly viper was so close paralyzed me. I couldn't move a muscle to pick up a rifle or even to call out and warn my uncle.

"The snake moved even closer, rattling its tail in warning and swaying its head, an evil luster gleaming in its eyes. Only a few strangled sobs escaped my throat."

Nancy wanted to close her eyes and cover her ears with her hands, but she couldn't resist listening to the rest of the story. After all, Ivor was still alive and had already lived to be an old man, so she knew he would make it through the crisis.

"My uncle heard my sobs and awoke. The instant he saw the snake, he grabbed his rifle, but the snake bit me. My uncle knew what to do to keep me alive till I reached the hospital." Ivor shook his head. "It wasn't pleasant to go through, but I survived."

"All's well that ends well," Helga quoted. "You must've had a guardian angel, too. This afternoon I was telling the girls about my sister and me being lost in the woods when we were little girls."

This launched Ivor into more storytelling, and the time passed quickly. Before they were ready, it was time to head for home again.

"Hurry up and get well fast," Dannie urged, squeezing Ivor's hand. "We need you back there in the hemlock woods. Wolf misses you, too. He's been howling for you."

Ivor chuckled. "Tell him I'm coming as soon as I can, and give him a hug for me."

"I'll do it tonight, as soon as I get home," Dannie promised.

And he didn't forget it. In the dim light of the shanty, Dannie thought he even saw Wolf grin and wag his tail ever so slightly.

14

How the Wind Blows

ON Monday morning when Nancy went out to the meadow to bring in the cow, the earth was sparkling with dew. She sucked in great breaths of air fragrant from the moist earth and the lush green grasses.

Nancy thought of Ivor cooped up in the hospital, not able to enjoy the beauties of spring. He had to gag on the odors of disinfectants and medicines and ether, instead of sniffing this heady fragrance. The birds were trilling as merrily as they ever had, it seemed. She sent a prayer heavenward for Ivor's speedy recovery, and for him to be able to come home to his beloved hemlock woods again.

After milking the cow and helping with the calves, she offered to feed the chickens so Dannie could get an earlier start in helping Omar. Nancy entered the range shelter with a bucket of mash and suddenly stopped short. Where were all the chickens? It had been over a week since she had last been out here, and then there were two dozen laying hens. Now she counted them—only fifteen!

Nancy stood staring at them dumbly. A few scattered feathers lay here and there, and a pile of loose dirt scooped up beside the west wall told the story. Some animal had tunneled under the wall and made off with the hens. Nancy set down her bucket of feed on the dirt floor and ran for Omar. Dannie came, too.

"Didn't you notice that the hens were disappearing before your very eyes when you fed them?" Nancy asked Dannie. "Or when did this happen? There are only fifteen left."

Dannie shook his head. "I-I was always in a hurry. I did notice there were fewer eggs, but I forgot to mention it. Helga doesn't eat eggs, so she wasn't needing any more while Ivor was in the hospital."

Omar began to examine the scooped-out place beneath the side of the range shelter. "I think it's the same culprit that killed Helga's lamb and Fisher's bunnies," he decided. "I've been hearing barks from the hemlock woods lately. It could be a stray dog. We'll have to make some more efforts to hunt it down. Meanwhile, we'll move the hens up into that little room on the second floor above the shop. The thievin' culprit can't dig in there."

Nancy pondered the situation while she filled the big copper furnace kettle in the washhouse. She built a fire in the furnace under the kettle. While the kettle was heating up, she poured in bucketsful of rainwater from the cistern pump. She gathered all the laundry and neatly sorted it in piles on the washhouse floor.

After she had dipped buckets of boiling water into the wringer washer, she called Dannie in to start the washing machine engine. She had filled the engine with gas before starting the fire, and he checked the oil before starting it.

"Have you ridden Andrew's horse already?" Nancy asked him.

"Not yet," Dannie shook his head. "He wants to ride and drive Silky Silas himself a few times first, to make sure he really is as well broken as the auctioneer said. I'll bring him over for you to see him as soon as Andrew gives me permission."

I hope Andrew'll offer to give me a ride, too, Nancy thought.

With two of Dannie's mighty jerks on the starter cord, the engine roared to life. While Nancy was hanging out the first load of the white Sunday wash on the line, to dry in the warm sunshine and breezes, her thoughts once again turned to the varmint. She hoped the men would soon catch it.

Nancy and Sally had been planning to get together one of these days to make noodles with the extra eggs, but now they would have to postpone that project. Omar and Nancy supplied the Fishers with their breakfast and baking eggs, and also Elmer's and Ivor's. They probably wouldn't reach around now with only fifteen hens.

"I think I'll go over to Fishers this afternoon and tell Sally," Nancy muttered. "We'll probably need to buy our noodles for awhile."

After the dinner dishes were washed, Nancy set out for the Fishers, taking along a few quarts of strawberries for them. They had plowed down their old patch this year and started a new one that wasn't bearing yet. As she had requested, Dannie had hitched Dandy to the pony cart and tied him to the ring under the forebay (overhang of the barn), ready and waiting for her to use.

When Nancy entered the Fishers' kitchen, Sally was bent over the washbowl, shampooing her long hair in sudsy water. "I always do this every Monday, so I can manage my hair again by the next weekend. For awhile after shampooing, it's so flyaway and wild that I can hardly keep the hairpins in my bob."

She rinsed her hair, wrung it out, patted it drier with a towel, and flung it around her shoulder. "Let's sit out on the porch so my hair can dry in the breeze. There are a few bucketsful of peas to hull, and you may help if you wish."

As they hulled the peas, Nancy gave her message about the noodles and told the story about the stolen hens.

"How awful," Sally declared. "I think it's time to call in someone with a few good hunting dogs to track down the critter. Over at the Shady Lane Tack Shop, they have a few dogs that could do that."

"You have a good idea," Nancy agreed. "I'll suggest it to Omar. By the way, how does Andrew like his new horse by this time? I noticed he didn't drive him to the singing."

"That's because he wasn't shod yet. He drove him through the field lanes, though, and said he has not one thing to complain about him yet. I suppose Dannie's getting impatient to try him out, too."

"Sort of," Nancy admitted. "But he's really growing up. You know, the first summer he was here, he was so . . . so—he had to have what he wanted and when he wanted it, or he'd go into a pout. He's not that way at all, anymore."

"Well, he went through a lot, too. When he said he'd like to call his horse Silas, I didn't remember right away that Silas was his dad's name. Andrew said I shouldn't have said what I did about calling him Silky," Sally said thoughtfully. "Oh well, he didn't seem to mind."

Changing the subject, Sally asked, "Did you know that a family by the name of Gardiner moved into the big house on the hill, over on the other side of Jacob's? It's been empty for a few years, but now we see lights in it every evening.

"Mrs. Davis told us that they're a couple who moved out from the city, and that the woman, Janine, is taking treatments for cancer. She's only thirty-two years old. They have no friends in this area, and they're not churchgoing folks."

"Poor woman," Nancy clucked her tongue sympathetically. "Do they have any children?"

"One school-age girl, and she's gone to live with her aunt in Detroit. Mrs. Davis asked if we'd like to go along to visit her sometime. Would you be interested in going along, too?"

"I think we should," Nancy agreed. "We could take her a casserole or offer to do some work for her. Oh, there's Andrew hitching up his new horse. Now I can see what he looks like in the harness."

"He must've taken him to the blacksmith first thing this afternoon." Sally set down the bucketful of pea shells. "Let's go out to the end of the walk, where we can see him better. Maybe he'll even offer us a ride."

When Andrew pulled up at the walk, he said, "If you want a ride home, Nancy, hop on. I'm going that way anyhow."

Nancy hopped up, and Sally was left standing there alone.

"Well!" Sally sputtered to herself as Nancy and her brother sped away. "So that's how the wind blows. I always thought so, but now I'm sure of it."

15

Tender Loving Care

SO, what will it be for everyday use, Silas or Silky?"
Nancy asked, reaching back to pull her Kapp in place
as the wind whistled past her ears. She hadn't both-
ered to wear a bonnet.

"I think I'll humor Dannie this time," Andrew
chuckled. "Say, look at that trot. Stylish would be a
more fitting name."

"He's upheaded, too," Nancy said admiringly,
"and no slowpoke."

As they neared the end of Omar's lane, a car came
over the hill. "Now we'll see whether he shies from
traffic." Andrew cleared his throat. "This will give
you a chance to decide whether or not you want to go
along with a horse like this, or rather with his master.

"Now that I have my new buggy and horse, would you, uh—"

He was interrupted by a gasp from Nancy. "The car!" she cried. "It's weaving from side to side. I think the driver's asleep!"

Andrew pulled hard on the right rein, and the horse jumped aside, but the car relentlessly came on toward them, though not at a high rate of speed. Nancy screamed. Suddenly the driver jerked awake and slammed on the brakes. But it was too late!

There was a sickening thud as he plowed into the horse's left shoulder, throwing him into the ditch. Nancy felt herself flying through the air. She landed, unhurt, on the grassy bank. A few feet away Andrew was picking himself up. The car door opened, and the elderly gentleman crawled out, trembling.

"I'm ever so sorry," he said in a quavering voice. "I must've fallen asleep. You people aren't hurt, are you?" His anxiety was written on his face.

"No, just shook up a bit." Andrew tried to smile, but only managed a weak grin.

"But the horse. . . . I don't know about him."

Omar and Dannie had been scything thistles in the meadow and had seen it happen. Both came sprinting toward them. Their faces relaxed when they saw that no one appeared to be hurt, no one but the horse, apparently. Omar quickly unfastened the harness and pushed the buggy away.

"I have a car phone," the elderly man said. "I'll call the police and the vet."

Dannie was kneeling beside the horse, stroking his

neck and talking to him in a soothing voice. Tears were streaking down his face. By the time the vet arrived, the horse was up but not putting much weight on his left front leg. He was trembling all over. There was a big gash in his shoulder, and the blood was dripping down his leg. There was no danger of him running away in that condition.

The vet examined him, then turned to Andrew. "I could stitch that gash, but there's danger of infection. We'd almost have to have him at the hospital to keep administering shots of antibiotics, and even then we might lose him. If the wound would heal, there's a 90 percent chance that he'd always be lame. His ligaments are torn or badly stretched and bruised. I'd advise you to have him put down now."

Dannie suddenly sprang forward, with clenched fists and blazing eyes. "No, no!" he shouted. "I won't allow it! He's my horse, mine and Andrew's. I'll take care of him and doctor him up. Someday I'm going to be a vet myself. . . . I won't let you kill him!"

The vet stood there, blinking in surprise at the lad's outburst.

Andrew cleared his throat. "Dannie, I don't like it either, but we must face facts. I can't drive a lame horse. The Humane Society would be out in a hurry. I—I don't know what to do."

The driver of the car spoke up. "I'm sure that my insurance company will pay for whatever you decide, whether it's the worth of the horse or the vet's bill."

The police car arrived then, and there were questions to answer and forms to fill out. In the end,

Andrew opted for the money he had in the horse, and then gave the horse to Dannie.

Now it was up to Omar as to what they would do with it, have it put down, or give Dannie the chance to doctor him back to health. Dannie would have to pay the vet bills if he kept him.

That evening after the cow was milked and the calves fed, Nancy went out to the horse stables to check on the golden horse. Dannie and Omar were watching as he pulled wisps of hay from the manger and nibbled at them. "See how much better Silas is feeling already," Dannie said brightly. "We stitched up the gash and gave him a shot of penicillin."

Omar mopped his forehead. "Dannie says 'we,' but look who's sweating. I never realized a horse had so many layers of muscle and skin. This may have been a foolish thing to do. If infection sets in . . . but I gave him the shot of penicillin, and sprayed the wound with Red Cote after I was finished."

"I'm sure Silas will be fine," Dannie asserted.

"Don't get your hopes up too high, Dannie," Omar cautioned. "The vet said he needs more shots of antibiotics so infection won't set in. If that happens— well, sometimes we just have to learn the hard way."

For the next few days, Dannie spent every spare moment in the barn with Silas. If TLC (tender loving care) would make him well, there would be no doubt of him getting better. At least half a dozen times a day, he rinsed the wound with peroxide and sprayed it with germ killer. He crooned and fussed over the horse, stroking his mane and patting his neck.

Dannie himself gave the horse the needed shots of antibiotics, promising to repay Omar for the cost. He never failed to bring Silas something extra to eat, such as tiny carrots from the garden or slices of dried apples from the pantry. In a few days, Dannie began to give the horse some exercise, leading him slowly around the barnyard morning and evening.

A few days after the accident, Nancy was sitting on the porch and hand-sewing a patch on a pair of Dannie's pants. Old Mrs. Davis' car came in the lane.

Sally got out and ran to the porch. "We're going to visit Janine Gardiner now—you know, the lady I told you about that has cancer. We're wondering if it suits you to come along. I'm sorry I couldn't let you know beforehand, but we didn't know for sure when it would suit us, either. Mrs. Davis just stopped in unexpectedly to take us along. If you want to go, just grab your bonnet and jump in."

"Sure." Nancy sprang up and in a minute reappeared on the porch with a quart of strawberries. She had picked them for supper but saw them on the counter and decided to take them along as a gift for Mrs. Gardiner. Nancy climbed onto the backseat beside Sally. Mrs. Fisher was in front with Mrs. Davis.

"We would've asked your sister Mary to go along, too," Sally said to Nancy, "but thought maybe it's better not to take children along. We don't know Janine's condition, and maybe the noise would be too much for her."

Nancy agreed. "Maybe Mary can go some other time while I babysit for her."

It was only a mile. Soon they were heading up the Gardiners' long, winding paved drive to the big stately old house on the hill. They rang the doorbell, and a white-capped nurse answered. After she met the visitors, she disappeared again and in a moment came back, saying that Janine welcomed them and invited them to come in to her room.

The house was old, but in earlier days it had been a grand mansion. They put their bonnets on the hall table and followed the nurse to Mrs. Gardiner's room. She was lying dispiritedly on a daybed, looking small and thin.

"Hello," she said, with a twinge of interest in her voice. "Are you Aye-mish?"

This started off a conversation, with Mrs. Davis and Mrs. Fisher doing most of the talking. But soon Janine began to talk about herself.

"We moved out of the city to this remote place without telling any of our friends where we went." She spoke in a weak voice. "I couldn't bear to have them see me like this. Oh, I hate it, just hate it, looking so thin and gaunt and old, and without hair." Her head was covered with a thin scarf.

"There, there." Mrs. Davis tried to soothe her. "You don't look all that sick."

"Oh, but I do," Janine cried. "I never wanted to look like this and be so ill. We went to a lot of different doctors, and they all told us the same thing: 'Without chemotherapy, you won't be here much longer.'

"I couldn't bear to tell my daughter, Jodie, or let her see me suffer. So we sent her to her great-aunt in

Detroit. She didn't want to go and even threw a fit and begged to stay here, but it was out of the question. Jodie couldn't understand why she had to go. I told her it was only for the summer. By fall, I should be through with my treatments."

"Why didn't she want to go?" Sally wondered.

"Uh . . . well . . . Aunt Kim is domineering. If she'd know my condition, she'd be here to take over. Besides, we aren't on speaking terms, so I can't even call her. I wish Jodie would call me, though. I can't understand why she doesn't. I told her I couldn't call her, and she'd have to call me."

Mrs. Davis asked, "Would you mind if I'd send our minister over to see you? We'd like to help."

Janine Gardiner shrugged her shoulders. "If you wish, but I can't see that it would do any good. We've never been churchgoing folks."

Mrs. Fisher clasped her hand and said, "We'll be thinking of you." That was her way of saying, "We'll be praying for you."

Sally and Nancy offered to help out in whatever way they could. Janine said she would let them know if she needed help. They filed out quietly, feeling sorry for the sick woman.

For the rest of the day, Nancy was in a sober mood. Never again would she take good health for granted. She couldn't imagine being so on the outs with an aunt that she couldn't even say hello to her, not even on the phone.

Suddenly Nancy was glad that from childhood she had been taught to forgive and not hold grudges.

16

Florabelle

DANNIE felt excited as he trudged through the hemlock woods on his way to Helga's place. For one thing, in a few days, or as soon as it suited them, Abie and his brothers were coming to these woods with their hunting dogs. They were going to track down the varmint that had killed the lamb, the hens, and the bunnies.

He was also happy that Silas, the golden horse, was doing so well. So far, there was no sign of any infection. With all the loving care and attention that Dannie slathered on him, he just *had* to get well.

Best of all, today Ivor was coming home from the hospital! Or rather, he was probably home already. Omar had given Dannie permission to go over right after dinner (the noon meal). He knew how anxious Dannie was to see Ivor.

Dannie quickend his pace. He could hardly wait to see the friendly old man that he had secretly adopted as his grandfather. After all, he had never known either of his real grandfathers.

As he rounded the bend at the first spring, he stopped for a tin of refreshing spring water, swallowed after chewing a few sprigs of mint. He decided, as always, that it was the best and purest water he had ever tasted. Dannie tossed an acorn shell at a chattering squirrel, then went on his way, using a crooked branch as a walking stick.

When he came into the clearing where the little abandoned cabin stood, a flash of blue up in the swaying hemlock branches caught his eye. An indigo bunting!

He was so absorbed in watching the bird that he failed to see the figure of a person hurrying out the cabin door and making a dive for the ferny underbrush. But a sharp bark drew his attention to it, just in time to see a flash of tawny gold and white, and a pair of blue-jeaned legs disappear into the brush.

"Hey!" he called, breaking into a run. He heard the thrashing sound of someone running through the thickets. By the time he reached the place, all was quiet. Dannie stood for a moment, debating about what he should do, torn between his desire to see Ivor and his curiosity.

He decided that he might have a long, tiresome chase if he followed, and the fugitive might have a good hiding place. So he reluctantly left. But he resolved that when Abie came with his hunting dogs, they'd scour every inch of the mountain and solve the mystery in the hemlock woods once and for all.

When Dannie emerged from the woods at Ivor's place, he caught the familiar sight of the shady porch with the old man sitting on his hickory rocker. Wolf was by his side. This scene brought a shout of welcome to Dannie's lips. He broke into a trot and in a few seconds reached Ivor's side and sank breathlessly to the porch steps beside Wolf.

"Well, well, happy day! If it isn't me Dannie boy," Ivor beamed, "Why, I think I'd dance a jig, but this bad knee of mine just won't allow it." His leg was propped up on a hassock, and pillows surrounded him on the rocker.

"You'll soon be good as new, I'm sure," Dannie said. "With Helga to take care of you, and me to do your work. . . ."

"Aye, I hope so. But it's these gastric ulcers that are giving me the most trouble just now. My dad used to say that goat's milk is good for the stomach. I just wish that somehow or other, I'd be able to get some goat's milk for a few weeks. Then maybe I would soon be good as new. But just wishing won't accomplish anything."

Dannie jumped up from the step so fast that Wolf sprang aside. "I know where I can buy goat's milk for you, and it's not far from here—just a mile and a half down the road. They're Amish people, and their name is Miller. I'll go right now." He was all eagerness.

"Great!" Ivor's eyes lit up. "If you have the time to go now, step inside and ask Helga for money to pay for it."

Helga was already at the door because she had heard their conversation through the screen.

"I'll go now," said Dannie, "since Omar gave me the afternoon off. I just wish Silas's shoulder would already be healed so I could ride over. But walking won't take all that long, either."

"Silas, who's he?" Ivor wondered.

Dannie took the time to tell the whole story and had Ivor's entire sympathy and attention. "I'll make you a jar of my special drawing salve," he promised. "It's made from a recipe handed down by the Indians, and it's better than anything you can buy. It'll draw the soreness right out of Silas's shoulder. I'll have it ready for you tonight."

"Your horse will be sure to get well now," Helga assured him. "Ivor's salve is potent stuff."

So Dannie was in high spirits as he trudged out the long lane, carrying a plastic gallon jug that Helga had given him for the milk. He hoped the goat's milk would be just as potent in healing Ivor's stomach.

At the Miller farm, Dannie knocked on the screened porch door. There was no answer, so he knocked again, louder. From somewhere in another room, a muffled voice finally called, "Come right in."

He stepped inside, blinking his eyes to adjust to the dimness. The shades were drawn, but he was able to see the old-fashioned furnishings: the old settee, the striped carpet runners, and the old antique sideboard and caned chairs.

"I'm in here," the voice called from the next room. "Come on over."

Dannie crossed the room and stood in the doorway. This room was brighter, with the window shades all the way up. An elderly woman, wearing a Kapp just like Nancy's, only larger, was seated at a quilt that nearly filled the room, busily stitching and quilting away.

"Hello," Dannie said timidly. "I came to buy some goat's milk."

The woman straightened up and adjusted her glasses. For the first time he noticed that she was on a wheelchair. "For that you'll have to go out and see Abner. He's probably out in the springhouse, down in the dip behind the barn." She smiled and added, "I think I know you. You're Omar Petersheim's *Gnecht* (hired man), aren't you?"

Dannie nodded as he remembered seeing her at church. He told her who the goat milk was for, then thanked her and made his way out to see Abner. Under the forebay of the barn, an old tan-colored dog lay sleeping. When he heard Dannie's footsteps, he opened one eye, greeted him by thumping his tail on the concrete, then went back to sleep.

The top half of the barn door was open, and a chunky old horse stretched his neck out through the opening and whinnied a greeting. The place was neat and well-kept. But way out in back of the barn, there were some shabby-looking goat pens, made of posts and chicken wire.

"Maaaa!" a querulous, wavering voice called out.

Dannie jumped back, startled, and then grinned. It was only a goat. He went over to the pen. In it was a nanny and two pert-looking little kids, with soft mobile ears and cute expressions on their faces. There were more pens, all with goats in them.

In one pen was a crafty-looking old billy goat. Dannie reached in and patted the curly top of his head between the two horns. A moment later, he backed away, holding his nose. He certainly had a strong, goaty smell. The billy goat's beard quavered and a deep-sounding "Maaaaaaa" came out.

Dannie headed for the springhouse, about a hundred feet out in the meadow, sunk in a dip so that only the roof was visible from the uphill side. A stone wall was built around it on three sides. Approaching the little building, Dannie knew that Abner was inside, for he could hear him singing the *Loblied* (praise song) in a quavery old voice.

He descended the old stone steps. "Hello," Dannie called to the old man bending over the clear running water. It was flowing from a pipe into a shallow trough, then out a small grated window at the other end.

The singing stopped, and the man straightened up in surprise. "*Verschreck mich net so!* (don't scare me so)," he exclaimed. "*Waer bisht du* (who are you)?"

Dannie quickly introduced himself and stated his mission. Old Abner had a flowing white beard and kindly eyes. Dannie's eyes were drawn to the interior of the springhouse. There were half a dozen big flat rocks in the water, and each rock held above the water a big circle of light yellow cheese in a press. Goat cheese! He figured that this springhouse had been someone's only refrigerator at one time. That made it all the more interesting.

A dipper hung on the wall beside the running water. After taking in everything, Dannie's eyes returned to the old man, who seemed to be debating something. "Can you milk a goat?" Abner asked, studying the lad in front of him.

"I—I never did," Dannie had to admit. "But I guess I could learn. Why?"

"Well, I was just thinking, maybe I could loan you Florabelle, one of my milk goats, for as long as this Ivan, or Ivor, needs the milk for his ulcers. That way I wouldn't need to milk her." His eyes twinkled.

"Sure," Danny agreed. "Ivor has an empty pen we could put her in. I'd like to learn to milk a goat."

Soon Abner hitched his plump mare to the spring wagon, which had a pen built on the back. Dannie found himself on the high seat beside Abner, with Florabelle maaing from the pen in back. They were headed for the little farmette in the hemlock woods. On his lap he held a big round of goat cheese wrapped in plastic, a gift for Ivor.

17

A Peacekeeper

IT was evening, and Dannie sat on the porch with Wolf, between Ivor and Helga, just like old times. They were sipping cold, refreshing mint tea and sampling pieces of Abner Miller's tasty goat cheese.

Dannie had just come in from milking Florabelle and finishing the chores. Ivor was sipping a glassful of still-warm goat's milk.

"Ah!" Ivor said, smacking his lips. "I can feel the healing. Yes, I can feel the healing happening." He closed his eyes blissfully. "Thanks to Dannie, and to Florabelle."

"And to Abner Miller," Dannie added. "He sure is a kindhearted old man."

"That he is," Ivor agreed. "We had a nice visit.

Sometime he'll come again and bring his wife along. I have a feeling we're going to be best of friends."

Dannie soon felt that Ivor was in a storytelling mood, and he was in a mood to listen, so he egged him on. "Helga said you had a great-grandfather who was a traveling preacher and that you know some good stories about him. Could you tell me some of them?"

"Sure can." Ivor was glad to have an audience. "My great-grandfather was sent out West to help keep peace between Indians and white settlers. The whites were taking the Indians' hunting grounds. Some bad traders were cheating them and supplying them with liquor, which the Indians called firewater because it put their brains on fire.

"Those white scoundrels were asking for trouble, and that's why parson Jedediah was sent." Ivor finished his glass of goat's milk and leaned back in the hickory rocker, stroking Wolf's glossy muzzle, resting on his knee.

"One night Jed was riding home rather late, feeling uneasy because a trapper had stolen his blunderbuss. He was in deep woods where wildlife abounded, and an Indian village was nearby.

"Jed heard some whimpering and found a little Indian child on the bank of a stream. Somehow the infant had toddled away from the village.

"Now he was in an awful fix. He knew if he left the child lie there, it would be at the mercy of wild beasts. But if he took the child to the village, he didn't know what the Indians would do to him because other whites had mistreated the Indians so much."

Ivor paused in his story to reposition his leg on the hassock. Helga brought out more mint tea and more slices of goat's cheese. Dannie helped himself and listened eagerly as the tale continued.

"Brave Jed followed his conscience and took the child to the village. Though he was afraid, he walked up to the braves sitting round the campfire. They took him captive. The toddler hadn't been missed yet, so maybe at first they thought he had stolen it. They tied him to a tree.

"The next morning, wide-eyed children stared at him. A young squaw, the mother of the lost child, brought him breakfast and treated him kindly. He had been feeling badly rewarded for his kind deed, done to keep the golden rule: 'Do unto others as you would have others do unto you.'

"In the end, he found another saying still holding true: 'Cast your bread upon the waters, and you shall find it after many days.' Yes sir, Dannie boy, you'll never be sorry for keeping the golden rule. I've proved that many a time, and I've always been sorry for the times I didn't treat others kindly."

Ivor sat thinking for a few moments, then went on with the story. "The braves of that Indian village sat in a circle for a council meeting. They were solemn and took turns puffing on a pipe while discussing something in loud tones. Jed knew his fate was in their hands.

"He also knew that the Indians admire courage and despise signs of weakness. So he tried not to show his fears. Suddenly the mother of the rescued toddler rushed into the circle, waving her arms and talking fast, raising her eyes in appeal to the chief and asking mercy for Jed.

"At first the warriors scowled, but then one by one they seemed to yield and nod their heads. Soon everyone relaxed. The council meeting was over. They treated Jed like the hero he was.

"For two months he was with the Indians. They became good friends and wanted to adopt him as their brother. So they plucked the hair out of his chin." Ivor chuckled. "Say, Dannie, did you ever see a picture of an Indian with a beard? They tell me that full-blooded American Indians don't grow beards—that's just the way God made them.

"Anyhow, they wanted Jed to be one of them, so they did their best to turn him into an Indian. Beside a stream, they set up a little steam tepee, willow poles covered with buffalo robes. Inside they built a fire in a circle of stones. With Jed inside, they poured water over the hot stones.

"Taking the steam bath and chewing sassafras roots and spicewood leaves were supposed to purify him and make him one with his Indian brothers. The toddler's mother made him a pair of moccasins, and her husband gave him a fowling piece for shooting small game."

Ivor paused, idly stroking Wolf's fur and watching the night winds quiver the leaves on the trees, then went on. "Jed became good friends with the chief and learned to talk with him. He told the chief that his mission was to get the whites to treat the Indians fairly. Finally they sent him back to his own people.

"Jed was well rewarded for his good deed in returning the child. After that, the Indians kept bringing his family gifts of buffalo meat and venison when he was away on his pastoral duties.

"Once when the whole family was sick in bed with a fever, the mother of the papoose came to their cabin to care for them. The squaw gave them Indian potions and herbs and likely saved their lives."

The story was finished. Dannie sat thinking about Jedediah and his adventures. The stars had come out, and the fireflies were flickering in the clearing.

Helga got up briskly and said, "Time for bed. I see Wolf is in dreamland already."

At the sound of his name, Wolf raised his regal head and rose to his feet. Dannie got his flashlight and secured Wolf in the shanty for the night. Then he made sure that Florabelle was okay and headed for his own bed, to dream of peacekeeper Jedediah and the Indians.

18

Two Escapees

THE next morning Dannie was up early to do his chores. Now he also had Florabelle to milk, and he knew that Ivor wanted another glassful of warm goat's milk before breakfast. He said it had to be taken warm, for that was part of the cure.

The birds were twittering to greet the light, and the glow in the eastern sky promised a fine day. Dannie waited till last to feed and milk Florabelle, so Ivor would be awake by the time he had the milk ready.

When he opened the gate to her pen, Dannie stared in stunned surprise. The pen was empty—the goat was gone. Probably it had run off into the hemlock woods. How had Florabelle managed to get out?

Dannie wanted to run in and tell Ivor and Helga,

but thought better of it. Maybe he could easily find the goat and bring her back. Then they wouldn't need to worry. But finding Florabelle wasn't as easy as finding Bessie the cow had been. The ground had dried off, and there were no tracks.

He walked out to the little cabin, over to the old dump, and then to the waterfall area, but didn't see a trace of the wandering Nannie. He walked all the way out to the first spring and to the place where Omar's lane entered the woods. From here he could see Omar's buildings, and he spied a big, shiny car parked between the house and the barn. There was Omar, motioning him in.

Dannie began to run. Maybe they had found Florabelle. He hoped she hadn't been hit by a car. He jogged all the way, puffing and panting, and slid to a stop near the car. A big, heavyset man with a florid complexion and not-so-friendly eyes stepped forward and extended a hand.

"So you're Dannie," he said. "I—I'm your Uncle Rodney. I've come to take you home with me. Your mother was my sister."

Dannie's eyes widened and his mouth flew open. The big man was speaking again. "I was in the area on a business trip and decided to look you up."

He lowered his voice. "Dannie, we can't have you living with these hillbillies. I'll do better than that by my dead sister's son. My wife and I live in Chicago, and you'll have a much easier life living with us. We have all the conveniences, TV, videos, and no one will make you a slave. You'll have lots of friends there."

Still Dannie was mute.

Omar, too, was speechless. He knew they had no legal claims on Dannie, even though he seemed like a real brother to them now. He felt sick at heart.

Finally Dannie found his voice. "No th-thank-you, sir. I'm not going with you." His voice was polite, but there was defiance in his eyes.

"I'm sorry, but you don't have a choice. "I'm your legal guardian until you're eighteen." He knew that wasn't true, but he was trying to convince the boy to come with him without a fuss.

"I'm driving this rental car. We're going home by jet, and we have to be on our way to the airport. Pack your things quickly, but don't bother to pack any of your hillbilly clothes—I'll buy you new ones."

When Dannie refused to budge, his uncle said, "Are you coming, or will I need to call the police?"

Dannie suddenly felt powerless and had a sudden urge to make off for the hemlock woods. That beefy man would never be able to catch him. But then he thought that the police would somehow or other track him down like they do bank robbers. Maybe they'd even send out a helicopter with a searchlight or put bloodhounds on his trail.

He felt beaten and trapped, unable to escape from this ruthless man. But then an idea began to form in his mind. He would pretend to cooperate and go with his uncle. But once there, he would escape, hitchhike home, and hide in the hemlock woods until his uncle forgot about him.

Not till he was flying high above the clouds in a jet

did Dannie remember lost Florabelle. What would Ivor and Helga do now? Then he thought of Silas, his golden horse, and began to cry. Without his care and Ivor's special drawing salve, he might die.

Uncle Rodney, as he had told Dannie to call him, was reading a newspaper and pretended not to notice the tears. Dannie concentrated on the view from the window and tried not to think of his predicament. He said a prayer and began to feel better. God had helped him earlier. He trusted that God would hear his prayer now and answer, in one way or another, as Mamm and Daed had taught him.

Landing at the airport was exciting, and the bustle of the big city captured his interest. Uncle Rodney's apartment was on the tenth floor of a big building in the suburbs. The first thing Dannie noticed was the plush and luxurious furnishings and decor.

Aunt Trish greeted him politely enough, but without a smile or any warmth in her tone of voice. She had not expected her husband to bring home a boy!

After hours of miserable tossing that first night, Dannie cried himself to sleep He was terribly home-sick. Here there were no animals, no fresh air laden with the scents of springtime, no birds singing, no farms and fields, no Ivor and Helga, and no Omar and Nancy. The food Aunt Trish had served for dinner, as they called their evening meal, had tasted like sawdust to him and had stuck in his throat.

When he finally fell into an exhausted sleep, it was close to the time when he would usually start with morning chores. But in the city, no roosters crowed or birds sang to awaken him. When he stirred, he could hardly believe that the clock said ten in the morning.

His uncle had given him a pair of blue jeans and a T-shirt to wear, so he put them on. Out in the kitchenette, he found a note on the counter saying that he could help himself to some breakfast and then watch TV, or do whatever he wished. The note said his aunt would be back at three o'clock. Then they were going out to shop for some "decent clothes" for him, she promised.

Dannie stood at the window, staring down into the busy street. From so high up, the cars looked tiny, as if in a world apart. "I must make plans," he mused aloud. "Let's see, I have the fifty dollars Ivor gave me, but that sure won't go far. Besides, I can't buy a plane ticket because Uncle Rodney could track me that way. What else is there to do?"

He felt like a caged animal, prowling around in the small apartment. Dannie had eaten little the night before and now felt hunger pangs gnawing. If he was to make a getaway, he would need some grub. He found a box of cornflakes and a carton of milk in the refrigerator. Eating a bowl of cereal whetted his appetite.

Bacon and eggs were in the fridge, so he soon had some sizzling in the pan, to eat with toast. The hours stretched out ahead of him, and he looked for something to do. By two-thirty, he could stand it no longer. He was in no mood to go shopping for clothes, so he decided to take a walk.

Dannie hoped that somehow or other, a miraculous way of escape would open for him. If so, he would want his Amish clothes again. He found them stuffed into a trash can, pulled them out, and carefully folded them into a shopping bag.

Since he had planned to escape, he had brought nothing but the clothes on his back, his wallet, his new flashlight, and his pocketknife. Uncle Rodney had stuffed the flashlight and pocketknife in his own suitcase for the flight and then had given them back to Dannie when they reached the apartment.

The elevator took him down in short order, and then he was out on the sidewalk, blinking in the bright sunshine. He began to walk eastward, according to the sun, not caring if he never saw Uncle Rodney and Aunt Trish's apartment again.

19

The Fugitive

WHEN Ivor and Helga heard that Dannie had been practically kidnapped, their dismay knew no bounds. Andrew and Sally, and Jacob and Mary, and the whole neighborhood and church district were saddened. Their hearts went out to Omar and Nancy, and to the rest of the Petersheim family. Many a prayer was sent heavenward on Dannie's behalf.

For three days Florabelle was missing, and then one morning she was mysteriously back in her pen, maaing to be fed and milked. Ivor and Helga were sure that someone had milked her those three days. What mystery! They did not know who it could have been. Helga decided that she could milk the goat now. Together, she and Ivor tended the rest of the animals.

Omar took over the care of Dannie's golden horse. With Ivor's good drawing salve, the danger of infection was soon over, but he was still quite lame. But now there was no one to bring him carrots and apples every few hours and to shower him with the TLC that Dannie had given. Andrew had bought himself another horse, a big black gelding this time. He was trying to summon the courage to ask Nancy a certain question again. If only that accident hadn't interrupted him.

• • •

When Dannie left his uncle's apartment, he began to walk briskly, ignoring the noise and the traffic. A plan was forming in his mind, a plan of escape. His only drawback was not having enough money. He would have to get a job somewhere and earn enough to get back to the Hemlock Hill Homestead. Hitchhiking would probably be too suspicious or even impossible.

A lumbering bus came to a halt at a bus stop. Passengers emerged, while others waited to get on. Dannie sprinted ahead and managed to get on before the door closed. As long as the bus headed east, he would stay on it. Bus fare wasn't all that expensive.

Several hours later found him on the street again. He had asked the driver for instructions and knew what bus to take next. Dannie was relieved to see it coming and then to be safely aboard. They were leaving the suburbs behind and heading out into the countryside.

When that bus came to the end of its route, and Dannie disembarked, twilight was descending. Here the houses were set far back from the road and had beautifully landscaped lawns, in a well-to-do area. He walked briskly eastward, as if he had a purpose and destination in mind, but actually he had no idea what he would do next.

The dusk was deepening, and lights twinkled on in the windows. Some children were in a backyard playing, shouting, and laughing together; Dannie felt forlorn and homesick. He wondered how Silas was doing and whether Florabelle had been found.

Just ahead stood a moving van by the roadside, where two men were loading furniture. As they headed back to the house, he heard one of them say, "Just one more piece, and then we're ready to head for Indiana."

Dannie's ears perked up. *Indiana!* If he could somehow hitch a ride there, he would be that much closer home. On a sudden impulse, Dannie stepped into the shadows of a tall hedge around the property. When the men disappeared into the house, he hoisted himself up into the truck and searched for a hiding place. Ah! There was a sofa, covered with an old blanket. Dannie quickly slid onto it, pulling the blanket and some clothing bags over himself.

The loaders came back and, with a heave and a grunt, put another piece of furniture on the truck. At the back, they tied some tall pieces of furniture to the walls, then slammed the rear doors of the truck. A few minutes later, the purr of the engine and the vibrations told Dannie they were on the move.

He had a comfortable hiding place. If it hadn't been for the worry of being discovered when the truck was unloaded, he would have felt better. He was afraid the police would be called. What would happen to him then?

After a while, Dannie slept, but it wasn't a peaceful, dreamless sleep. It was more like dozing fitfully, then jerking awake countless times. Always, the hum of the wheels told him they were still on the move. Once when he awoke, the truck had stopped, and Dannie tensely waited for the doors to be opened. But nothing happened. About fifteen minutes later, they were going again. *Probably stopped for gas and coffee*, Dannie decided.

The same thing happened again, and this time the stop was much longer. Dannie again went through the agony of suspense and thought, *Maybe they're eating a meal*. Eventually the truck was moving again, and Dannie slept.

The next time Dannie awoke, his throat felt parched with thirst and hunger pangs plagued him. He wished the truck would stop and the men would open the doors, no matter what the outcome. When he got his wish, he was tense and afraid. He made sure he was entirely covered with the blanket. If only he could somehow manage to get away without being seen.

He steeled himself as the doors were flung open and morning sunshine streamed in. "Made it in record time," one of the men was saying. "Here, give me a hand with this table." With a grunt and a heave, they lifted the heavy table, and the sound of their footsteps receded on the sidewalk.

Dannie peeked out from under the blanket. The coast seemed clear, so he quickly stretched his legs and got up. As soon as he saw the men toting the table disappear into the house, he crawled off the truck and strode briskly away, toward the rising sun.

He was in a small town. Just ahead, he spied a gas station and a small cafe, and into this he went, glad to be off the street. Dannie ordered bacon, an egg-and-cheese biscuit, and a cup of hot chocolate. When the waitress at the counter gave him a friendly smile, he gathered the courage to ask her, "Are there any Amish farms in this area?"

"Oh yes!" she replied. "You're practically in the heart of Amish country. Just stay on this road heading east, and you'll see them all around you."

That was good news for Dannie. He was sure he'd be able to get work on a farm this time of the year. After finishing his breakfast, he eagerly set out, heading into the country. It was a sparkling morning, and Dannie felt immensely thankful to be seeing farmland all around him instead of city streets.

There was hardly any traffic. When he came to a small bridge spanning a stream, he crawled under the fence into the meadow. Under the bridge, he changed from his city togs into his Amish clothes.

He looked longingly at the winding creek and the patch of woodland into which it flowed. It would be great to do some exploring there. But he knew he must go on and find himself a job, so he could get home to the hemlock woods. There he would be safe till Uncle Rodney would give up looking for him and forget about him.

After another mile of brisk walking, Dannie rounded a bend where the road ran through a grove of trees. There on the other side, about five hundred feet ahead, was an Amish farm! Yes, it had to be an Amish farm: no electric lines were running in to the buildings, and a windmill was pumping water.

Dannie quickened his pace, his heart beating fast. Would he have the courage to walk in and ask for work? Just the thought of it made his knees feel weak. What if they wouldn't trust him and would report him to the authorities?

Swallowing his fear, Dannie bravely turned in toward the farmhouse. There was a white board fence on either side of the lane, and cows grazed peacefully in a meadow on the right. At the end of the lane stood a big barn and silo, and on the left stood another big shed. He followed the lane as it wound between these buildings. Then he could see the big farmhouse, with gray siding and an L-shaped porch.

For a moment he stood still, debating whether he should go first to the barn or to the house. A movement near the front door caught his eye. A big German shepherd dog stood up and suddenly came bounding out toward Dannie, barking fiercely.

20

Ebony in Stride

NANCY'S heart felt heavy as she bent over the long rows of pea vines in the garden. She was pulling out the old vines, picking the few remaining pods from each stalk, and throwing the pods into a bucket. There had been a shower last night, and once again the world was washed clean and sparkling.

The birds seemed to sing all the more for it. A white-throated sparrow trilled from the rose thicket. Breezes were wafting delightful scents here and there, scents of roses and moist earth and growing things. But Nancy's thoughts were on Dannie. Whatever would become of him now? Would they ever see him again?

Last night she dreamed he had come back but hadn't been the same. He had turned into an urban hippie, jeering at Omar and Nancy and calling them hillbillies. Nancy had awakened feeling simply awful, and even now she shuddered as she remembered it. But then she recalled what Mamm had written in her letter: "It is better to pray than to worry." Yet it wasn't easy to keep on praying in faith.

There! The last pea vine was out, and Omar would drive through with the horses and wagon and fork up the piles. Nancy hurried to the house with her bucket of peas, stopping at the pump to wash her muddy feet. She had promised to do some cleaning today for Janine Gardiner, the woman who had cancer. Already she was late.

Sally and Nancy were taking turns going and helping Janine once a week, as a favor for her. Omar was working on Jacob's farm today and would eat dinner there. Nancy set the bucket of peas in the cool cellar and caught herself thinking, *If Dannie were here. . . .* He had loved to help *blick* (hull) peas, and would gladly have sat under the shade tree and *blicked* them for her.

Hurriedly she donned a clean apron and grabbed her bonnet. She would have to walk to the Gardiners, for Dandy had lost a shoe. By the time she reached the Gardiners and walked up the winding drive to the big house, she was momentarily tired. Janine Gardiner met her at the door, looking much better, but with a scarf tied around her bald head.

"Hello, Nancy. It's so good to see you." There was genuine gladness in Janine's welcome. "You're bright and early."

"Early?" Nancy hid a smile. She thought she was late. "It's nice to see you looking so much better." Nancy was amazed at how Janine had changed since the last time.

"I *am* better," Janine agreed. "The chemotherapy is doing its work. All along, the doctors gave me a good prognosis. I just found it hard to believe I would get better. I'm glad I don't need my nurse anymore.

"Now, sit down for a bit. I'll get you a cup of tea and a few cookies. You've been walking a long way."

"Thanks," replied Nancy. "Just what I need."

"There's just one cloud on the horizon today." Janine sat down on a chair and grimaced. "My mother-in-law is coming and staying for a week. I just know she'll take over completely while she's here because she's that type. Even Jeff, my husband, can't stand up to her. I think he's still tied to her apron strings. Oh well, it's just for a week."

"That snack was delicious," Nancy said. "Now I'm ready to work, whatever you want me to do."

"Here, I'll show you what needs to be done. We can't have Mother Gardiner finding any dust."

A couple hours later, Nancy was on her hands and knees washing the kitchen floor when she heard the front doorbell ring. Janine went to the door. "Hello, Mother." Nancy heard her say cordially. "Come right in. Jeff will bring in your luggage later."

"Where's Jodie?" the older lady asked first thing. "I've got something for her."

"Uh, she's with Aunt Kim for a few weeks." Janine's voice sounded apologetic.

"Your Aunt Kim?" Mother Gardiner asked sharply. "I thought you weren't on speaking terms with her."

"That's true. But I simply couldn't have Jodie here while I'm sick and losing my hair like this. I couldn't stand to have her see me this way."

"Posh! Fiddlesticks!" the older lady said scornfully. "What nonsense! So does Jodie like it there? From what I remember of your Aunt Kim, she seemed quite domineering."

Janine sighed. "It's just for this summer," she said in a small voice.

"Does Jodie like it there?" Mother Gardiner wasn't to be put off lightly, and there was force behind the question.

"I—I don't know—I haven't called her." Janine cringed at the look on her mother-in-law's face.

"What! You haven't talked to her since she's there? I'm going to call and find out this minute. What's her number? If she's not happy there, I'm going to have her sent home immediately. You're getting better fast."

"No!" Janine's voice sounded hurt and angry at the same time. "I don't want her here till my hair grows back! I haven't told her that I have cancer."

Nancy couldn't help but listen as the battle of wills raged on.

"Fiddlesticks!" Mother Gardiner said again. "Doesn't this younger generation have any . . . any . . . gumption? Well, are you going to give me her number, or aren't you? Jodie deserves to know about this and to come home if she wants to."

In the end, Janine gave in and found her aunt's number. Mother Gardiner called her immediately. Only a few words had been exchanged when suddenly she shrieked and dropped the receiver. She picked it up and shouted into the phone, "Are you sure? She hasn't arrived there? You know nothing about it? Sakes alive!"

It was like pandemonium breaking loose. Turning on her daughter-in-law, Mother Gardiner fairly shouted, "Jodie never even arrived at Aunt Kim's. They never even knew she was planning to come."

Janine sank weakly into a chair. "But . . . but . . . Jodie told me she called and asked if it was okay. She said it was . . . and that Aunt Kim wants her to come. I can't believe she fibbed!"

"That shows she didn't want to go." Mother Gardiner's voice was accusing.

Janine wearily got up, came into the kitchen, and told Nancy. "As soon as you're done washing the floor, you may go. With Mother Gardiner here. . . ." There were tears in her eyes.

Janine went back to her guest. "My daughter probably went to one of her friends back home in the city. She hated to leave them to come out here to live. Calm down, Mother. Jodie's not lost. We'll call all her friends. No—I think I know which one she's with. There's no need to worry."

Nancy quickly finished her cleaning, got her bonnet, and left quietly. She was glad to get out of there and to walk home in peace. *The Gardiners have their share of troubles, just like we do*, she thought wearily. But she couldn't understand how Janine could not be on speaking terms with her aunt—so much so that she couldn't even as much as say hello on the phone. It was downright discouraging.

So engrossed was Nancy in the Gardiners' troubles that she didn't hear the sound of hoofbeats and the rattle of buggy wheels. Suddenly she heard a voice saying, "Whoa, Ebony. Nancy, do you want a ride home?" It was Andrew, with his new horse hitched to the buggy.

"I'd be delighted. Dandy needs to be taken to the blacksmith shop for a shoe, so I had to walk. How do you like your new horse?" Nancy was glad that at least her voice sounded natural even though she felt flustered.

"He's a man's horse—he needs more miles. If I could drive him ten miles every day for a while, he'd tame down pretty fast. He's a bit skittish yet and rarin' to go."

"Did I hear you call him Ebony?" Nancy asked.

Andrew chuckled. "Yes. This one has papers, with three or four names. *Ebony* was the easiest to pronounce. Oh, by the way, do you mind if we go the long way round to Ivor's other lane and make a stop there? I borrowed a drill bit from him that I'd like to return. Or maybe you're in a hurry?"

"Oh no, I'd like that," Nancy said truthfully. "I was planning to help Janine Gardiner most of the day, and Omar will be getting his dinner at Mary's table." She went on to tell him of the Gardiners' troubles.

"Hmmm," Andrew sympathized. "That sounds a

little like Dannie's case. He didn't want to go to his uncle, and Jodie didn't want to go to her aunt, or great-aunt. It sure is hard to understand, though, why anyone would be so crabby as to avoid speaking to a relative."

"They must not believe in forgiving each other," Nancy suggested.

Andrew's mind wasn't on the conversation, though. He was wondering when would be the best time to put an end to this small talk and ask Nancy that all-important question. But Nancy, remembering what had happened the last time she had gone with Andrew, felt somewhat rattled and chattered away as a cover for her feelings.

Ebony trotted swiftly onward. In what seemed like in no time at all, they were trotting into Ivor's lane.

21

The Long Way Home

NANCY hadn't often come in to Ivor's place this way. She gazed rapturously at the towering, arched hemlock branches overhead and took deep breaths of their spicy fragrance. Halfway in the lane was a low bridge with wooden railings, spanning a small brook. Here Ebony balked, eyeing the strange contraption warily, snorting with dread.

Andrew gave the lines to Nancy, got off, and led him across. Then they were on their way again at a fast speed. Ebony wanted to get away from the bridge as fast as he could. Beside the lane, a bobwhite hen, trailing a row of little fluffy chicks, was startled and dashed for cover with her brood trailing her.

Moments later, they heard a series of sharp, yelping

barks from somewhere in the hemlock woods, followed by the long-drawn-out "Awa-awa-oooh-oooh" of Ivor's wolf.

"I don't think I'll ever get over having the chills when I hear that," Nancy confessed. "Somehow, those quavering echoes dying away tingle my spine. But what was that barking?"

"Let's ask Ivor." Andrew guided Ebony into the clearing and tied him to a fence.

Ivor was sitting at his usual spot on the shady porch, on his hickory rocker, and welcomed them warmly, glad as ever to see then.

"No word from Dannie boy yet?" he asked first thing.

Nancy shook her head, and Ivor's hopeful look turned cloudy with sadness. Helga had joined them on the porch, as happy to have visitors as Ivor was. It would never do for the visitors to rush off right away.

"Did you hear that barking in the woods just now?" Ivor asked. "We keep hearing that every once in a while, and Wolf answers with a howl. Somehow, I think it has something to do with the killings that have been going on lately. It might be a stray dog. What's happening about getting those hunting dogs in on the case?"

"Not much," Nancy had to admit. "I guess we forgot about it, distracted when Dannie left so suddenly. At least our hens are safe now."

"For a while, I thought it might be a bobcat," Ivor said. "There hasn't been a bobcat in these woods in the last ten years or so. Maybe one sneaked back.

They do travel far. But the way your hens were taken reminds me more of a dog than a bobcat. And those barks from the woods sound like a dog's."

"Ya well, at least it's not a panther," Andrew joked. "We haven't heard any big cat screaming."

"Well, I sure heard them when I was a boy out West with my uncle," Ivor said. "If you ever hear a panther scream, you won't think Wolf's howl so scary anymore. It's a wild cry that just about tears the air with ear-splitting ferocity. It rises to a snarling crescendo, then slowly dies away in quivering, heartrending screeches.

"Did I ever tell you about the tangle my great-grandfather Jedediah once had with a panther and a bear?"

"Maybe a long time ago," Andrew answered. "But I'd like to hear it again." He knew the old man loved to tell stories and that it was his favorite pastime.

Ivor leaned back in his rocker, thinking of the long-ago days. "My dad used to tell us this tale, but much more vividly than I can. At the scary parts, he kept his listeners trembling with worry."

Ivor launched into the story. "One day my great-grandfather Jed took his muzzle-loader and gunpowder and went into the woods to bring his family a fresh supply of venison. After a while, he felt uneasy and thought it strange that he had traveled so far without seeing deer.

"After he shot a few squirrels, he realized he had gone far enough into strange country. So he headed for home. The birds ceased singing, and a hush and gloom settled over the forest. An eerie feeling of being watched caused him to shudder.

"He whirled around. There, not twenty yards away, was a huge grizzly, standing upright and watching him with small glittering eyes! Bellowing with rage, the grizzly came galloping toward him.

"Jed barely had time to shoot, but he aimed and fired. The roar of the muzzle-loader didn't seem to slow the bear. Jed scrambled up the closest tree. Its trunk was about six inches thick and had few hand-holds. In his haste, he dropped the gun.

"Now Jed was sure he was dangling just above the jaws of death. But the bear had an injured front foot and couldn't climb. It charged the tree trunk, clawing with its good front paw and shaking the tree. Poor Jed held on for dear life. The bear tore up the forest floor, pausing now and then to glare at Jed.

"Later the grizzly settled down under the tree, with moans and groans now and then. Twilight descended on the woods till all Jed could see in the black of night was the red of the angry bear's eyes. Around midnight, the grizzly was restless and wandered off. Jed waited for what seemed like hours, then let himself down from the tree.

"As he bent to pick up his gun, he thought he heard a 'Woof!' Jed sprang up the tree faster than he had come down, making sure to hold onto the gun this time.

"A new spine-tingling sound reached his ears, the unearthly scream of a hungry panther. The screams closed in, coming from one side and then the other.

The big cat was stalking him. Jed strained to see into the thickets, but the night seemed to be black as pitch.

"Hearing those fearful screams was terrifying enough. But when all became deathly quiet, the silence was unbearable." Ivor paused, enjoying the horror written on the young listeners' faces. Helga calmly went on crocheting.

"Since Jed couldn't see the panther, he had no way of knowing how or when he would pounce. When the clouds blew away from the face of the moon, Jed was horrified to see the monster crouched twenty feet away, in another tree, and slightly above him.

"Jed aimed for the blazing yellow eyes of the feline fiend, and his shot hit its mark. The beast tumbled down dead. When dawn broke, Jed skinned the panther and started for home, reaching it safe and sound. He lived to show off the panther hide and tell the story to his great-grandchildren."

When the story was finished, Helga jumped up. "It's lunchtime, and I have a big kettle of beef stew simmering on the stove. You must come in and eat with us."

Nancy looked at Andrew. After all, he was the driver.

"It sounds mighty inviting, especially since I have to be my own cook today," Andrew admitted. "Mom and Sally went to visit Grandma Fisher. But the harness shop is open this afternoon, and I must get back to wait on my customers. Thanks anyhow."

Helga wasn't satisfied with this. In a few minutes, she came bustling out of the house, carrying two jars of stew, one for Andrew and one for Nancy. She also handed over a chunk of goat's cheese for each, brushing aside their thanks as if her gifts were nothing.

"Let's all remember to pray for Dannie," she reminded them as they headed for the buggy. "He's in our thoughts all the time."

They assured her they would as they waved.

"They're such a kind and friendly old couple," Nancy marveled. "We couldn't wish for better neighbors."

"Mmmm, hmmm," Andrew said absently as he untied Ebony and climbed into the buggy.

Nancy glanced at him. Apparently he had already forgotten Ivor and Helga and had something else on his mind.

After they turned onto the road, Andrew said, "Nancy, you know the *Yunge* (young folks) in the Summerville West district are having a Sunday evening singing in two weeks. I'd like to take you to the singing, if you don't mind. I think Ebony will really be in stride by then."

"Oh," she replied, "I'd like that. Anyhow, Omar will be taking Sally, so that would work out fine."

"Good." Andrew grinned, happy that he finally had the answer he wanted. "When we get there, I'll drop you off at the house, then tie up Ebony, and come inside for the singing. Afterward, I'll bring my rig up to the house, and when you see us, you can come right out. We'll try to get away before the boys make too many jokes at our expense."

"Ya, they'll make fun of us," Nancy responded. "But it's only words, and they mean well."

So it was settled before they reached Nancy's home, going the long way round. Andrew and Nancy would have their first real date for the singing on that Sunday evening.

22

Real Luxury

DANNIE stood rooted to the spot as the big German shepherd came running at the trespasser, growling and barking. The barn door opened and a man called out, "Quiet, Queenie. *Leg anne* (lie down)."

The dog slunk away, and the man walked over to Dannie. "*Waer bischt du* (who are you)?" he asked in a friendly tone of voice.

While he was walking in the lane, Dannie had decided that the best policy would be to tell the whole story, leaving nothing out. If he would be too secretive, others would become suspicious. But he wouldn't say he was going to hide in the hemlock woods, only that he wished to earn money to go home.

When Dannie was finished with the speech he had

rehearsed, the Amishman seemed to be pondering the situation for a few minutes. He pushed a small stone around with his foot. Then he straightened up and smiled.

"My next neighbor to the south, Ora Stutzman, has hired a van to start for Holmes County, Ohio, tomorrow morning. His dad is in the hospital with a heart attack, and they want to visit him. He told me it's going to make him quite busy to go just now, but the visit can't be postponed. He would probably have work for you to do today. If the van's not already promised full, you might even be able to catch a ride to Ohio. That would bring you nearer home."

"Oh, that would be great!" Dannie's eyes were alight. He thanked the man. After receiving exact directions to the Stutzmans, he headed out the lane with an eager spring to his steps. When he reached the road, he checked the name on the mailbox: Amos Shetler. He would say that Amos Shetler suggested that he inquire for work at the Stutzmans. Then he would likely have more of a chance, he figured.

His hopes were high as he trudged the half mile to the next farm. He found it without any trouble. The meadow here was dotted with black-and-white Holstein cows and heifers, and Dannie took the time to count them. Nearly fifty! No wonder Ora was almost too busy to travel at this time of the year.

The farm looked prosperous and as neatly kept as the Shetlers' place. Beside the house, a woman wearing a Kapp was hoeing in the garden, and two little girls played in a sandbox under a shade tree. Dannie gathered courage and walked over, ready with his planned speech. "Hello," he said bravely, and launched into his story.

The woman looked hot and tired, rubbing her back as she straightened up. She eyed him quizzically as he spoke. When his speech was finished, she smiled and said, "I believe you are telling the truth, but we'll have to see what Ora thinks when he comes in from the field. The van traveling to Ohio isn't filled yet, and I do need help here in the garden.

"If you could man this hoe for me this forenoon, I can at least give you dinner, all you want. More than that I can't promise. Ora will have to decide."

He politely thanked her, took the hoe, and went to work. This was something Dannie surely knew how to do, and he was careful to do a good job. The two little girls had come to stare at him and stand beside their mother as she picked peas. Then they went along to sit under the shade tree and help hull them. They were dressed much like Mary and Jacob's Nancy Ann, with hair fixed the same way.

Dannie vigorously swung his hoe the rest of the forenoon, ignoring the hot sun and his aching back. He was glad when Lizzie Stutzman went into the house to prepare dinner, but he half dreaded and feared Ora Stutzman's verdict. He swung between hope and despair, praying that Ora's response would be favorable. *My, that would be so good if I could go along to Ohio*, he thought.

Finally he heard the dinner bell ringing and saw Ora coming to the barn with his wagon and horses to unhitch. Two little boys were with him. He saw Lizzie go to the barn to talk with her husband, and saw them both glance his way. Dannie kept on hoeing, trying to calm his fears.

Then Ora was walking toward him, eyeing him keenly, and inspecting his work. "Time for dinner, Dannie." His voice was friendly. "It looks like you've done a good job in the garden and earned your meal. You can wash here at the pump before you go in."

They entered the kitchen, and the delicious smells set Dannie's mouth to watering. It seemed like a long time since he'd had a good home-cooked meal. The two little boys sent furtive glances his way but were too shy to speak to him.

On the table was a big platter of home-cured ham, a dish of mashed potatoes dripping with butter, fresh peas out of the garden, and a lettuce salad. There were freshly baked rhubarb pies, too, and a dish of strawberries. Dannie did full justice to the food.

After the family gave thanks again after the meal, Ora leaned back in his chair and told Dannie, "Ya, it seems to me like you are sincere. You worked hard in the garden. If you'll help me in the fields this afternoon and evening, I'll gladly give you a bed tonight and pay your way on the van to Ohio tomorrow."

Dannie wanted to clap his hands for joy, but he constrained himself, graciously smiled, and thanked Ora.

"I'll have the driver drop you off at my uncle's place," Ora went on. "He has a bulk-food store and can use your help there till you find a ride to Summerville."

Dannie's spirits soared. This sounded too good to be true. He had been worried about where he would go in Ohio. Now it was all planned out. That afternoon he worked with a will at helping to bale hay. In the evening he helped to milk the cows. Many times he had helped Jacob and Joe in their dairies. The fact that he knew how to go ahead with the cows would have convinced Ora that he was telling the truth, if nothing else had.

After the milking, there was more hay to bale. By the time Ora showed Dannie to the spare bedroom, he was bone weary. But he was happy, glad that it wasn't like last night on the sofa in the truck, or the miserable night before, at Uncle Rodney's place.

He sat at the screened window for a few minutes, listening to the frogs bellowing from the pond in the meadow, and the chirping of a few night birds in the treetops. It gave him a twinge of homesickness, and he longed to see all his loved ones again.

Dannie wondered how his horse, Silas, was doing, and if anyone was giving him the care he needed. What had happened to Florabelle, and how were Ivor and Helga taking his sudden departure? How Dannie wished to see them all again soon.

There was a tap on his door. Ora stuck in his head, saying that the bathroom across the hall was empty now and he could take a bath. That afternoon Lizzie had washed his Amish clothes, while he wore his jeans and T-shirt, so that he would have clean ones for tomorrow.

After his bath, the soft bed with clean, sweet-smelling sheets felt like real luxury. Dannie thanked God for the kindness of the Stutzmans and for care and protection thus far.

23

The Born Naturalist

WHEN thirteen-year-old Jodie Gardiner's mother had told her that she was to spend the summer with her great-aunt Kim, she was indignant. In the first place, she had not wanted to move out into the country near Summerville, away from all her friends. But when her dad told her she could have a dog there and study nature all she wanted, she reluctantly went along with the move.

Her parents took her to the animal shelter, and she chose Ginger, a beautiful tawny-and-white collie. During her few weeks of living in their new home, Ginger was the spark of her existence. They spent most of their time together outdoors, roaming the fields and woodlands.

Jodie had chosen to be home-schooled this last term. She finished the courses early, so she was free to do as she pleased—until her mother told her she had to live with Great-Aunt Kim for the summer. At first Jodie threw a fit, but when she saw her parents weren't going to yield, she used another tactic. She pretended to agree, though all the while she had no intention of going.

She faked a phone call to Kim and told her mother it was okay for her and Ginger to spend the summer there. Jodie insisted on traveling by herself. Her mother hired a taxi to drive her to the airport—on the very first day of her mother's chemotherapy treatment, which Jodie didn't know about. As soon as her parents left "for a doctor's appointment"—actually, for the hospital—Jodie called and canceled the taxi.

Jodie took Ginger and the camping gear she had been gathering and hiding under her bed. She also strapped on a backpack filled with trail food and dog food for Ginger. The two of them set out for the woods. Whenever she would need more food, she had plenty of money to buy it at the little Four Corners grocery store.

What she didn't have in the backpack, she stowed in the carriers of her bicycle, including her sleeping bag and flashlight. Ivor and Helga weren't home when Jodie pedaled through their lane, with Ginger running alongside, and trekked into the hemlock woods.

Jodie was delighted to find the little abandoned cabin in the clearing. At first, she thought she would set up housekeeping there, but then decided that others would find her there too easily. Next she decided to put up a little shelter with hemlock boughs, just big enough for her and Ginger. She had her Girl Scout knife and in a surprisingly short time had built a well-hidden and sturdy little house.

She covered the floor with the soft, springy tips of hemlock boughs and was reveling in the delightfully fragrant and spicy scent of her new abode. Then she heard Ginger barking excitedly from some distance away. After she hurried over to the spot, she found the dog digging furiously at the side of an embankment, making dirt clods and stones fly.

There was a thin slab of rock leaning against the grassy slope, and hard beside it was a bunny hole—Ginger's reason for digging. Suddenly a shower of dirt and small stones descended upon Ginger, and she quickly backed away. Jodie leaned down, looked into the gaping hole, and gasped. It was a good-sized cave, not just an animal lair.

She tilted the slab of rock forward, which widened the cave's doorway and let more light into it. The floor of the cave was paved with thin slabs of rock, and its sides and ceiling were layers of solid limestone. Above the entranceway was another slab of rock, keeping the surface soil on the embankment from sliding down or washing away. Ginger had merely widened the cave's opening a bit.

Seeing that the structure of the cave was solid and that it was safe to explore, Jodie delightedly crawled in, wide-eyed with wonder. It was like a little room, about ten feet wide and five feet high. In one corner stood a rickety old table and chair, both too fragile to use. On a rock ledge above it was a rusty tin box.

Jodie eagerly took it down, wondering what it might contain. But try as she might, she could not budge the rusty clasp. In exasperation, she put the box back on the ledge.

The rest of the small cave was bare. Right away, Jodie began to make plans for furnishing this excellent hideaway for herself and Ginger. Back she went for more hemlock boughs. They would make an excellent carpet for the stone floor.

At the dump she found the rusty little round table, and the old iron porch rocker that Dannie had once used in the abandoned cabin. This furniture she placed in the center of the cave. She covered the table with the vinyl imitation-lace tablecloth she'd bought at the Four Corners store.

Jodie discovered a nearly invisible trail that led through the hemlock woods and emerged at the road, just a mile from the store. She kept her bicycle hidden in a thicket near the road. Every few days, she made a trip to buy supplies. Since she was a newcomer in the area, she counted on the fact that others didn't know her.

The first week after she had claimed Ginger, they had once met Ivor and Wolf out on one of their rambles. Ivor had let her pet Wolf, assuring her that she wouldn't be harmed. More than once, she had heard Wolf's eerie howl but hadn't been afraid after their introduction.

After Jodie and Ginger set up housekeeping in the

cave, she avoided Ivor's place for fear she would be recognized. She often watched Dannie walking through the woods in the morning and evening, while she kept herself and Ginger carefully hidden. Several times she had almost been discovered. Jodie had built the rock waterfall that Dannie saw by the spring, when he plunged down the nearby embankment into Ginger's sleeping place one night.

With her binoculars, she spent hours watching the birds and wildlife in the woods, discovering their nests and lairs, and watching them feed and train their young. She was a born naturalist. There in the woods, she discovered her calling and decided to pursue related courses in college.

Even though she loved nature, she still grew lonely. When two Amish girls traipsed merrily through the woods, she looked longingly after them, wishing to make friends with them. Even with Ginger's companionship, she at times grew desperately lonely for the sound of a human voice.

Once a nanny goat visited them at the cave and stayed for three days. Jodie figured out how to milk her, giving some of the milk to Ginger and pouring the rest away. She didn't care to drink the warm goat's milk herself. Then the goat disappeared as mysteriously as she had come, and Jodie felt a new degree of loneliness.

She longed to go back home but didn't dare, for fear she would be sent to spend the rest of the summer with Great-Aunt Kim. But spending the summer here in the hemlock woods began to look less appealing to

Jodie every day. So she began to cast around in her mind for another option.

Because she wanted to keep Ginger, she couldn't go back to her friends in the city. One evening as Jodie was sitting by the waterfall, watching the clear water plunging down into the pool, she began to feel so frustrated, lonely, and abandoned that she burst into tears.

Ginger crowded close to her side, but Jodie wasn't so easily comforted. She sobbed until she was exhausted, and then she fell asleep with her head on a rock.

24

Dannie's Return

THE ride in the van seemed long and tiresome to Dannie, especially since he didn't know anyone except Ora Stutzman, who sat in the front seat with the driver. When he reached his destination in Ohio, Dannie had a mixture of gladness and shakiness as he crawled out of the van to face a new life situation.

By the drive, a big sign set in a bed of petunias advertised STUTZMAN'S BULK FOOD STORE. A small Boston terrier came out, yipping frantically. The screen door on the porch slammed, and elderly Eli Stutzman, with a salt-and-pepper colored beard, came out to greet them with a warm smile and handshake.

Ora would get his supper here, too, and then he

and his Uncle Eli would go to the hospital to visit Ora's dad. Eli's wife, Feenie, was a jolly, bustling, and motherly sort of person who made Dannie feel at home right away. She told him he could sit on the wooden swing under the shade tree while the menfolk visited until supper was ready. Skippy, the terrier, jumped up beside him, wiggling all over with delight at being invited onto his lap.

At the supper table, Dannie was happy to see a cup of mint tea on a saucer beside his plate, just like the tea that Helga served, except that it was hot instead of iced. There was also potato soup with parsley in it, and slices of homemade cheese that reminded him of the Millers' goat cheese. Homemade crackers went with it, followed by strawberry shortcake.

After supper, they toured the bulk food store. The Stutzmans showed Dannie what his work would be in the next few days, until an opportunity arose for him to travel with someone to Summerville.

In the store's office, Dannie's eyes widened at the sight of a fat potbellied pig rising to its feet. It grunted softly, expertly nosed open the screen door, and headed outside. The comical sight brought him a few laughs, but he soon learned that the pig was perfectly clean, housebroken, and well trained. He even suspected that the pig was bathed every day.

Dannie was tired from traveling and glad to be excused from working that evening, aside from helping Feenie Stutzman cap some strawberries for making jelly. Eli showed him to his bedroom early. He slept well all night and woke up at Eli's call.

The store required much work, such as weighing and bagging flour, sugar, rice, and assorted beans and grains. Dannie sliced and packaged lunchmeat and cheese, swept aisles, and bagged and carried groceries for the customers. Eli was a kind man to work for, and Dannie tried his best to do a good job.

He enjoyed the work, yet with great joy he hailed the news on the fourth day of his stay at the Stutzmans: tomorrow he would have a chance to travel with a vanload to Summerville. Maybe by tomorrow he could be back in the hemlock woods, and see at least some of his animal friends, if not the people.

Dannie planned to keep carefully hidden for a while to reduce the danger of Uncle Rodney kidnapping him. How long that might be, he didn't know, but he suspected it might take the rest of the summer. That night he was nearly too excited to sleep.

The van was coming early, so Feenie had packed him a lunch before bedtime and put it in the gas refrigerator. If no one else was up, he was to help himself to breakfast. But when his alarm clock jangled the next morning, and Dannie hurriedly dressed and went down to the kitchen, both Eli and Feenie were up to see him off. The gas kitchen lamp was lit, and scrapple and eggs were sizzling in the pan on the stove.

"You've been a big help to us here in the store, Dannie." Eli, still in socks without shoes, went over to his desk. "You've earned more than your room and board." He handed three twenty-dollar bills to Dannie and patted him on the shoulder. "You're welcome to come back any time."

Sixty dollars! Dannie was so thankful for it. He'd been worrying about what he'd have to eat while he camped in the hemlock woods. Maybe he could somehow disguise himself and buy food at the Four Corners store. Perhaps he could make the money last until fall.

Feenie gave him a business card with the store's name and address on it, and urged him to write to them when he safely reached home. He promised to write sometime, secretly doubting that he'd be able to do it right away.

Then the headlights of the van were turning in the lane. Dannie made his good-byes and was off, this time traveling with all strangers. Except for the driver of the hired van, the rest were all of one family, headed to their married son's place in the western end of the Summerville area.

Omar's place was in the eastern end, so Dannie would have to walk or hitchhike part of the way home. He thought it was best this way anyhow, not landing in the Petersheims' church district. The folks there wouldn't see the Petersheims on Sundays and ask Omar about Dannie's homecoming.

The Ohio family did some shopping on the way, and so it was high noon when they reached their destination. A meal was ready and waiting for them, and they persuaded Dannie to eat with them before setting out on his own. "After all," he told himself, "I had an early breakfast, and it might be my last home-cooked meal for a long time."

After dinner, Dannie rested under the shade tree

with the visiting menfolk, then started off in the early afternoon, telling them that it wasn't all that far. After all, what was fifteen miles compared to the hundreds of miles he had already come?

After walking for several miles, a friendly old man in a blue sedan stopped and offered to give him a lift. Dannie accepted gratefully, and this ride brought him within seven miles of Omar's place. Later, after walking four more miles, a motherly looking lady in a black car gave him another lift, taking him right to the road that passed Ivor's long lane.

Here Dannie used caution, ducking into the woods whenever he heard a horse and carriage coming. Everyone around here would know him and give his secret away. His excitement knew no bounds at being so close to home. It seemed like ages since he had seen them all. He wondered if Silas, the golden horse, was still alive, and if anyone had found Florabelle.

Dannie skirted around Ivor and Helga's place, stopping in a shady dell to eat the lunch that Feenie Stutzman had sent along. He had forgotten all about it at dinnertime, and now it came in handy for supper, after all that walking. There were thick bologna-and-cheese sandwiches, a banana, chocolate chip cookies, and peanut butter crackers.

All this made him thirsty, so he headed for the nearest spring. Here the spicy hemlock scent was strong, and Dannie took deep, delightful breaths of the fragrance. He pinched off a chew of mint and drank the sparkling clear water gratefully. He hadn't tasted such good water in all the time he was away.

Passing Ivor's place again, he looked longingly in that direction but headed for the secluded dell where Nancy loved to picnic. Here he could see all of Omar's farm. Tears stung his eyes at the sight. It made him even more homesick than he'd imagined it would.

Dannie headed back into the woods, deciding to console himself by going for an icy cold swim in the pool, under the waterfall. But when he rounded a bend in the trail and came in sight of the waterfall, an astonishing sight made him stop in his tracks. There beside the pool was a girl, fast asleep and slumped over a rock, with her head down on her arm. He stood there, transfixed at the sight, noticing her woebegone appearance and the tearstains on her cheeks.

Then a series of sharp barks echoed through the woods from some distance away. The girl awoke with a start, blinking her eyes in bewilderment, as surprised at seeing Dannie as he had been to see her.

25

As an Alien

WHEN Ginger came bounding over to her mistress, growling at Dannie, the moment of silence was broken. "Lie down, Ginger," Jodie commanded. "He won't hurt you." She turned to Dannie. "You won't tell on me, will you?"

"Tell on you? Not if you won't tell on me!" Dannie smiled at the girl. Before they knew it, both had introduced themselves and were telling each other their stories. They sympathized with each other, glad to have someone to confide in. Jodie showed Dannie her secret cave home.

Bit by bit, the mystery of the strange goings on in the hemlock woods was solved. Dannie had to laugh at himself for being frightened by a girl and her collie.

When the sun's rays were slanting sharply through the hemlock trees, Jodie looked at her watch and announced, "It's time to visit my fox family. Do you want to come along?"

Dannie nodded. "Sure. Sounds interesting. Do you mean there's a family of foxes living right here in the hemlock woods?"

"Come and see." Jodie put the unwilling Ginger into the cave and set the slab of rock in place, commanding the dog to stay put. "Let's see, the wind's from the west. That means we have to approach from the east side, so they won't catch our scent."

She led the way through the thickets for what seemed like several miles to Dannie, who had already done a lot of walking that afternoon. Jodie turned and laid a finger on her lips. "Shhhh! We're getting close. Now we have to proceed as quietly as Indians."

After sneaking slowly the rest of the way, Jodie carefully parted the boughs of a low-hanging hemlock and motioned Dannie forward. There on a rock stood a magnificent red fox, with a long bushy tail. It had its nose to the wind, sniffing the breeze and alert for any sign of danger.

Dannie stood motionless, hardly daring to breathe, awed at the scene. Soundlessly, moving like a shadow, the fox jumped from the rock, leapt down on a smaller pile of stones, and disappeared for a few moments. Then the fox reappeared and again carefully sniffed the wind, warily watching for any sign of danger. Dannie fervently hoped the wind wouldn't suddenly shift and give them away.

Moving cautiously, the fox slunk into a crevice in the rock wall and a few minutes later reappeared, followed by four little red foxes with black noses, also sniffing the wind. Dannie thought it was the cutest animal family he had ever seen.

After making sure it was safe, the little foxes began to scamper around, gnawing on old chicken bones that lay scattered around their dooryard. They growled to each other and pretended to fight for the bones, tumbling over each other, while the mother fox sat and watched with a benign expression on her face.

After awhile, Jodie's knee began to feel cramped, and when she shifted her weight, a twig snapped under her foot. Instantly the four little foxes vanished into the den, followed by their mother, the white tip of her tail disappearing last. So Jodie and Dannie quietly sneaked away, not daring to talk until they had left the fox den far behind.

"Those chicken bones," Dannie told Jodie. "Now I know what was stealing Omar's chickens. I expect the mother fox killed Ivor's lamb and Fisher's bunnies, too."

"Well," said Jodie, "somehow she has to feed her little ones, and nobody ever told her not to take farm animals."

"I guess that's right. Wolf's racket probably scared her off without the lamb. Thanks, Jodie, for showing me the fox family. I've never seen fox kits before. I hope nothing ever disturbs or harms them."

Back at the cave, Jodie showed Dannie the rusty old tin box. "I've tried my best to open this, " she told him. "But it's either locked or rusted shut. I'm dying of curiosity to see what's inside. This cave must've been someone else's hiding place a long time ago, and maybe what's in this box would give us a clue."

Dannie took the box outside and found a good-sized rock. "Mind if I bust it?" he asked.

Jodie said no, and Dannie began to pound at the clasp, wielding the rock with all his might. Finally the rock smashed it loose. Using his biggest pocketknife blade as a pry bar, Dannie forced the box open. The hinges groaned and squeaked as they gave way. He carefully lifted off the lid while Jodie watched in suspense.

"Gold nuggets!" he teased, watching Jodie's eyes pop. Then grinning, he opened the lid wider, and his own eyes grew big. "Arrowheads! A whole collection of them, and they all seem to be in perfect shape. What a find!"

"Stones," Jodie said in disgust. "I was hoping so much it would be valuable jewels, maybe a pearl necklace or gold earrings and a diamond bracelet."

"Oh, but these are arrowheads and probably worth a lot, too," Dannie assured her. "We must take them to Ivor, since he would know about such things. He's the one with the pet wolf."

"Well, all right. You may have them if you wish. I guess we'll never know who had a hideaway in the cave and collected them." She found herself a perch on a fallen tree, with Ginger at her side. Dannie sat on a rock, examining and admiring the arrowhead collection.

They talked until the dusky twilight descended, and

the stars twinkled overhead in the sky. The fireflies appeared, like magical little lanterns, and the swamp frogs began to croak. Soon the darkness thickened and settled into the woods, and a screech owl began to hoot.

Jodie shivered. "I don't like to be out in the woods much after dark. Ginger and I usually go to bed before it gets this dark. Are you going to sleep in the cabin?"

"Probably. But I want to do some exploring first. I'd like to wait up until Omar and Nancy are sleeping, and then go and see my golden horse. Maybe I'll even go to see Wolf."

"Okay, good night." Jodie whistled for Ginger and started carrying the box into the cave. "See you in the morning," Jodie called back. "Don't leave without telling me, because these woods are going to seem lonely without you."

"I won't," Dannie promised. He watched as the girl and the dog disappeared into the darkness. Then he rambled over to Nancy's picnic dell and sat on the fallen log, watching until the lights went out in Omar and Nancy's house. He waited for what seemed like an hour longer, to be sure they were asleep.

Then with his flashlight in hand, he headed in the field lane toward the barn. It gave him an odd feeling to be home and yet to feel so much like an alien. Slowly and cautiously he opened the barn door. Soft, sleepy whinnies from the horses greeted him.

There in the first stall was Silas, looking fit as a fiddle. Dannie affectionately stroked his mane and patted his neck, then ran his hand carefully down over the sore shoulder. Silas winced a bit. When Dannie moved him around in the stall, he could tell that the horse was still lame. But knowing that Silas was still alive and that infection hadn't set in was enough for Dannie now.

Seeing a pile of loose straw beside the horse stables, Dannie suddenly felt an irresistible desire to curl up on it and rest for a few minutes. He had promised Jodie he wouldn't leave the hemlock woods without telling her, but surely it wouldn't hurt to nap for a few minutes after all those miles he had walked today.

Dannie felt perfectly happy and comfortable, curled up on the sweet-smelling straw. Before he knew what had happened, he was fast asleep, lost in the land of sweet dreams.

Suddenly he awoke with a start, groping for his flashlight. He knew he had to leave now or next thing it would be morning. Omar would find him here, sleeping in the straw, and his plans would be spoiled.

Carefully he opened the barn door, then remembering Silas, he went back to hug him good-bye. Dannie went out into the night, carefully closing the barn door behind him.

26

Home to Stay

HEADING across the Hemlock Hill, Dannie decided to visit Wolf yet before he bedded down for the night in the little cabin. The midnight moon was shining overhead, and everything was peaceful. The hemlock woods were home sweet home to him after being so far away.

All the night sounds seemed friendly, and the walk to Ivor's clearing didn't seem far. As he crossed the clearing, on a sudden impulse he shone his flashlight into the goat pen. Yes, there was Florabelle, sleepily blinking her eyes. It gave Dannie an all-is-well feeling to see her safely back.

He carefully opened the shanty door without making any noise, knowing that Wolf wouldn't bark and give him away. But the effusive greeting that the big shaggy beast gave him was more boisterous than Dannie had planned on, and he tried to shush him up. Finally Wolf quieted down, and Dannie curled up beside him, resting against his solid flank.

Traipsing back to the cabin now did not appeal to Dannie. The thought of sneaking upstairs into Helga's spare room was tempting, just as napping had tempted him at Omar's, but he knew that was out of the question.

Suddenly he sat bolt upright, his heart beating fast. Dannie heard a door squeaking opening and the footsteps of someone coming. He looked about wildly for a place to hide. Just then, the shanty door opened and the light was snapped on, blinding Dannie momentarily.

"Dannie!" Ivor cried joyfully. "You're back! I knew it had to be you. No one else could have sneaked in here to Wolf like that. Where were you all this time?" He limped over to Dannie, using his cane. Behind him, Helga appeared, looking ghostly in her long white nightgown, but smiling happily.

"Tell us all about it," Ivor said, sitting down on the wood chopping block.

Finally Dannie found his voice and told the whole story from beginning to end. He even explained his plans to hide in the hemlock woods until Uncle Rodney would forget about coming for him.

"I have good news for you, Dannie," Ivor said happily. "Your uncle Rodney notified your dad that you had disappeared. Your dad came over and talked to

Omar. He said that if you showed up here, Omar was to tell you that you don't have to go with your uncle Rodney if you don't want to, since he has no real claims on you.

"Your dad said your uncle's claim to be your legal guardian was just a bluff. Your dad gave permission for you to stay with the Petersheims, if that's what you want to do. He told your uncle that, too, so you have nothing more to worry about from him."

Dannie heaved a sigh of relief. "I'm the gladdest of glads to hear it. That means I'm home to stay."

They all went into Helga's kitchen. While they sat and visited for another hour, she served crackers, goat cheese, and glasses of mint tea. Then they went off to bed, to sleep the last few hours of the night. Dannie was blissfully happy, and so were his dreams.

He awoke at dawn, to the happy singing of the birds. Right away he thought of Jodie and hurried to the hemlock woods. Dannie found her sitting by the waterfall, with Ginger at her side, at the very spot he had found her last night, still looking somewhat forlorn. He pitied her, having to stay alone in the hemlock woods.

A sudden idea flashed into his head: "Why don't you come with me to Ivor and Helga's house? You can trust them to the uttermost, and I'm sure they won't give you away. You could help them care for their animals and milk Florabelle for them. You'll be safe there, and so will your secret. Please come."

Jodie thought it over and finally agreed to go, remembering how lonely the woods had seemed when

Dannie was gone. "Can Ginger come, too? If she can't. . . ."

"Of course," Dannie promised. "Once she and Wolf get to know each other, there shouldn't be a problem. You'll love Helga, and Ivor, too." Dannie had no doubts about that. "They're the kindest, grandest old couple I ever knew."

Thus it happened that Jodie and Ginger came to live with Helga and Ivor. They took to each other right away and became the dearest of friends. Jodie consented to calling her parents. She told them where she was, and they immediately came to Ivor's house, rejoicing that their lost daughter was safely found.

Even after her mother was well again, Jodie spent a lot of time at Ivor and Helga's house. The kindhearted old couple and Jodie shared a desire to be friends with animals. They were a good and steadying influence on the young girl.

After Dannie had safely presented Jodie to Helga and knew she was in good hands, he immediately headed for home, to see Omar and Nancy. In the calf barn, Omar was mixing the milk replacer, and Nancy was getting the buckets ready.

The door burst open, and Dannie came in. "I'm home!" he announced happily.

For awhile it seemed like they were all talking and laughing and exclaiming over Dannie at once. He had to repeat his story for them and answer their questions. Then he just had to go and see Silas again.

As soon as the chores were done, Nancy went into the house and began a letter to Mamm and Daed. A week from Sunday, they were planning to come out to the Hemlock Hill Homestead, but they deserved to know the good news as soon as possible. Omar went to tell Jacob and Mary, who came over right away to see Dannie. They helped with the rejoicing, and the group laid plans for a family outing.

They decided to have their annual summer picnic for the *Freindschaft* (relatives) early this year, to celebrate Dannie's homecoming. This would be a week from Sunday, when the entire Petersheim clan was coming for a visit anyhow. It would be too early for watermelons, but cherry cobbler would do well, along with homemade raspberry ice cream.

After Jacob and Mary left, Nancy harnessed Dandy, hitched him to the pony cart, and headed out the lane. She was thankful for Omar's kindness in letting her go to tell the Fishers the good news. Nancy knew Omar would have enjoyed seeing the expression on Sally's face as much as she would enjoy telling Andrew that Dannie was home to stay.

27

The Family Picnic

SINCE the day of the picnic was warm, the coolness of the hemlock woods would feel just right. This was their district's Sunday with no church, so they could make an early start for the woods, before the heat of midday.

Joe and Arie arrived first, and Nancy dashed out to the buggy to bring Michael and baby Dorothy into the house. Next came Jacob and Mary and their family. Their youngest, baby Mary, was the same age as baby Dorothy, so Nancy had her fill of holding *schnuck Buppelin* (cute babies).

By midmorning, the van bringing Mamm, Daed, the boys, Susie, and Lydia arrived, and after that she had to share the babies. Lydia had a cast on her arm.

She had broken her wrist when she fell from a ladder while picking cherries. So that was one less rival because Mamm had cautioned Lydia not to carry the babies around while wearing a cast.

Andrew and Sally arrived soon afterward. The day wouldn't have been complete without them. Omar hitched the two workhorses to the big farm wagon. Everyone loaded their casseroles and Tupperware containers of eats, along with the freezers of ice cream, and hopped on for a ride into the hemlock woods.

"We're having the picnic at Ivor's house this year," Omar announced. "They prefer not to walk out to the cabin this time, but we can explore all we want after the picnic. "Ready, everyone?" He snapped the lines and ordered, "Giddap."

"Oh, these delightful hemlock woods," Sally blissfully declared as they rode under the trees. "There's no sound to compare to the sighing of the wind sweeping through the branches."

"Neither is there a fragrance to compare to that spicy scent of the hemlocks," Nancy remarked. "Nor to the flavor of the pure spring water along with some mint."

When the wagonload drew alongside the first bubbling spring, Andrew jumped down and brought a cupful of the sparkling water to Nancy, and even had the sprig of mint for her.

"I think I can take a hint," he winked at her. After she drank it empty, he ran to replace the cup and then easily caught up with the plodding workhorses before they turned the bend in the ferny trail.

Dappled sunshine dotted the trees, and chattering squirrels scolded the trespassers from branches overhead. A cottontail darted away, startled by the noise of the wagon. Just as in other years, this was a happy family occasion that would remain in their memory for years to come.

Rounding the next bend, Dannie called out, "There's Ivor, Helga, and Jodie. Look, they already have the big table set up in the yard."

"It's nice that the mystery in the hemlock woods is solved," Jacob commented.

Everyone agreed.

Being there in the woods, surrounded by the love of this big, caring family, gave Dannie a feeling of security and overflowing happiness. This year there was even more to be happy about, or maybe it just seemed that way.

Now he realized what it felt like to be parted from them and stranded far from home. Then too, Dannie had made a new friend—Jodie. His golden horse, Silas, though still lame, was on the road to recovery. Ivor was gaining strength after his knee replacement. All in all, Dannie thought, his world seemed to be coming together well, and to be blessed by God.

Not till lunch was over and the tables cleared did Helga notice the cast on Lydia's arm. She wanted to know what had happened. When Lydia told her, Helga said not a word and hurried into the house. Soon she came out carrying a colorful cardboard box.

"I have just the thing for you," Helga said. "A farm safety game, designed especially for youngsters who live on a farm. I found it at the bookstore in town last week. When I saw that the name of it was 'Amos and Sadie's Farm: A Pathway to Safety,' I couldn't resist buying it. I'll show you how to play it."

This caught Dannie's interest too, and he jumped up from where he was sprawled on the grass, listening to the menfolk talking. "Here's a place to spread the game board," he said. "This large, low tree stump is just right. C'mon, Jodie, you can help, too. Susie and Lydia, you take the other side."

The grown-ups gathered around to watch while Helga explained the directions. There were several stacks of farm safety question cards, and the players took turns picking a card. If they could answer correctly, they rolled a pair of dice to determine how far they could travel on the game board's spaces.

Dannie went first, and Helga read the question aloud to him. "What is the best way to protect your animals from rabies?" His quick answer was correct: "Have them vaccinated."

Jodie's turn was just as easy for her. "What carries Lyme disease?" "Deer ticks."

Lydia's question brought cheers from the audience. "True or false? Ladders can be dangerous?" Had Helga selected it on purpose? For the answer, Lydia waved her broken wrist in its cast.

Susie knew how to handle the next situation posed. "When operating on public roads, must buggies obey all traffic laws?" "Of course."

Later the questions became harder. When Lydia was asked, "What causes a rotten egg smell?" she quickly replied, "A rotten egg left over from a banty hen's nest." The correct answer was "hydrogen sulfide gas, a dangerous gas from a manure pit."

But even Jodie knew the answer to the query, "What should you do before going into a cow's stanchion to milk her?" "Speak to her first, so she is aware of your presence and doesn't kick."

One true-or-false statement really fit half the family. "Men with long beards should be careful around farm equipment." This brought some good-natured ribbing for Joe, who had once gotten his beard caught in a drill press.

When Dannie landed on a red HAZARD space on the game board that said, "Climbed into a bull pen," he had to go two spaces backward. Susie had to retreat one space when her red HAZARD block said, "Uh-oh! Went swimming alone. Move back one."

The game was fun and interesting. Even the grown-ups were learning from it and were reminded of farm safety precautions. They spent a happy hour playing it.

With the fun and fellowship of family and friends, the day passed quickly. Ivor was also telling interesting pioneer stories. All too soon it was time to pack away the leftover food and head for home.

At first Jodie had stuck to Dannie's side, but soon she was mingling with the rest of the family, feeling almost as at home among them as Dannie did.

"You know what?" Dannie heard Omar saying to Andrew. "We never did get around to bringing in hunting dogs to track down that thievin' varmint that got some of my chickens."

Dannie winked at Jodie, glad that it had been forgotten. That fox family had been so cute.

After everyone had left Omar's place and they had done the evening chores, Nancy hummed to herself as she got ready for the singing. She no longer dreaded the thought of Omar getting married and of having to leave Summerville—not after her little chat with Mary, who invited her to come and live with them any time.

Nancy watched out the window as Omar headed out the lane with Beauty hitched to the buggy to pick up Sally. The singing would be in the Summerville West district, so they needed to leave early.

A short time later, Andrew came driving in the lane with Ebony hitched to his new buggy. She waved to Dannie as she headed out the walk. He was currying his horse, Silas, until his glossy coat shone almost like real gold.

"If that horse doesn't recover completely, it won't be for lack of TLC," Andrew commented as Nancy got on the buggy. "He goes at it wholeheartedly."

"That's for sure," Nancy agreed. "He plans to even sleep out there on the straw tonight—at least until we come home from the singing."

"He's quite a boy, Dannie is," Andrew said, chuckling. "He'll do what he sets out to do in life."

Not till on the way home from the singing did Nancy open the subject of what she and Mary had talked about that afternoon.

"You know," she confided to Andrew, "I used to be almost dreading the day when Omar and Sally will get married. I figured I'd have to leave Summerville. But now, this afternoon Mary asked me to live with them after Omar doesn't need me for a housekeeper anymore. So that's a load off my mind."

"That's wonderful," Andrew said. He was thinking, *Silly! It wouldn't have gone long anyway until I'd have asked Nancy to be my housekeeper.* But now was yet not the proper time to say it.

Unaware of Andrew's thoughts, Nancy was happily musing, *To think that one time I declared I'd never be talked into moving away from our dear Whispering Brook Farm, not even to keep house for Omar. How things can change if we give up our selfish wills and let God work things out for good.*

Notes and Credits

Chapter 1. "The best is yet to be." Robert Browning.

Chapter 5. The "Loblied (praise song)" is sung second in the Amish Sunday church services; no. 131 in the *Ausbund*.

Chapter 6. The Lord's Prayer is found in Matthew 6:9-13.

Chapter 7, 12-13, 17, 21. The tales of pioneer days are adapted from *The Lost Children of the Alleghenies*, by Charles R. McCarthy (Huntingdon, Pa.: Brethren's Publishing Co., 1888); and *Golden Rock*, by Edward Sylvester Ellis (New York: American Publishers Corp., 1896).

Chapter 17. The golden rule is found in Matthew 7:12 and Luke 6:31.

Chapter 17. "Cast your bread upon the waters" is from Ecclesiastes 11:1.

Chapter 27. The questions and answers on farm safety come from a board game, "Amos and Sadie's Farm: A Pathway to Safety" (1999), available from Clay Bookstore, 2450 W. Main St., Ephrata, PA 17522 (717-733-7253). The game was developed through the initiative and leadership of Kathleen Fisher, a Penn State professor of nursing. Its initial production was sponsored by the Strasburg (Pa.) Clinic for Special Children and the Lancaster County (Pa.) Safe Kids Coalition, aided by a grant from the Salt Lake City Children's Miracle Network. A committee of Amish and Mennonites are keeping it in print.

Chapter 27. Romans 8:28 refers to God making all things work together for good, as clarified in the *New Revised Standard Version* and its footnotes giving alternate readings.

The Author

THE author's pen name is Carrie Bender. She is a member of an old order group. With her husband and children, she lives among the Amish in Lancaster County, Pennsylvania. Her books are listed on page 2.

Bender is the popular author of the Whispering Brook Series, books about fun-loving Nancy Petersheim as she grows up surrounded by her close-knit Amish family, friends, and church community. This series is for children and a general audience.

The Miriam's Journal Series is also well appreciated by a wide reading public. These stories in journal form are about a middle-aged Amish woman who for the first time finds love leading to marriage. Miriam and Nate raise a lively family and face life with faith and faithfulness.

Miriam's Cookbook presents recipes for the tasty, hearty meals of Amish everyday life. They are spiced with fitting excerpts from Bender's books.

The Dora's Diary Series, also in journal form, tells about Miriam and Nate's adopted daughter going out with the young folks, becoming a schoolteacher, and growing close to a special boyfriend.

Herald Press (616 Walnut Ave., Scottdale, PA 15683) has received many fan letters for Carrie Bender. Readers say they have "thoroughly enjoyed" her "heartwarming" books. Her writing is "like a breath of fresh air," telling of "loyalty, caring, and love of family and neighbors." They give "a comforting sense of peace and purpose."

Library Journal says, "Bender's writing is sheer poetry. It leads readers to ponder the intimate relationship of people and nature."